Welcome to Hiptoun

PJ Kropp

Contents

1 From the Bush to the Big Smoke

On a warm and partly clouded day, Charlie Murdoch Ash drove his modified 1970-model khaki-green Land Rover from the small town of Ratatatatutra to the large city of Covidorne, just over four hundred kilometres away. Covidorne is the capital of the Austrutopian state of Luzerstan.

The 'antiquated' vehicle cruised down the dual-carriage freeway at leisurely speeds of between 80-95 kilometres per hour (where the speed limit was 110 kph) and remained in the left lane for the entire trip, overtaken by all other vehicles – even large trucks.

Charlie's family resided a few kilometres away from the small town of Ratatatatutra and owned what used to be a dairy farm. Several years earlier, the farm had reached a point where his parents considered dairy farming no longer economically viable. This was due to a significant reduction in milk prices offered by the large dairy manufacturers and major supermarket chains.

Throughout the next few months, the family managed to earn what may be considered a 'basic income' primarily from *water trading* as they possessed limited water rights on their large property.

During this time, they gradually transformed a section of the former dairy farm and redeveloped it into a small orchard by planting trees of cherries, peaches, plums, pears, and apples.

Additionally, they managed to create a livestock farm that included cattle and sheep, a small number of pigs, and a large well-ventilated coop of egg-laying chickens.

Charlie eventually reached the dazzling northern outskirts of Covidorne. He then drove along Kiddenee Road (a major thoroughfare in the capital city) for twenty kilometres before reaching his destination: the suburb of Hiptoun.

After turning off Kiddenee Road and driving along two side streets, Charlie stopped before a block of units. The building complex was named the *Spirit of Wokeness.*

Charlie had secured a one-bedroom unit on an online accommodation rental website three weeks earlier. He drove his 'retro-mobile' (a term popularised by the local inhabitants upon the occasional sighting of a decades-old vehicle in the neighbourhood) into the residential carpark, underneath the unit accommodation. It was now almost 2:00 p.m.

Carrying a small luggage bag, Charlie walked to a nearby elevator. Inside, he pressed a button that took him to the second level.

A few minutes later, Charlie greeted the real estate agency representative who, in turn, handed him the keys to open the door of unit number six. This unit was one of eight units in the accommodation complex.

The one-bedroom unit, although small, was still spacious enough to meet Charlie's accommodation needs. Importantly though, the unit contained several essential items of furniture: a double-sized bed; a well-used lounge suite; a coffee table (that could also be used as a leg rest), and four wooden well-used chairs surrounding a small dinner table. He decided to use the bedroom as a part-study room as well.

Two days later, Charlie purchased a custom-designed computer table that accommodated the following: a desktop tower, a monitor, two small speakers, a large keyboard, and a modem.

Charlie went back to the underground carpark to retrieve the rest of his belongings, walking back and forth several times. The parking facility contained eight parking spaces but only three were occupied by motor vehicles.

Besides Charlie's Land Rover, there were two other motor vehicles: a small pink-coloured (and shiny) Volkswagen Polo and a heavily rusted, multiple-dented grey Toyota Camry.

Every allotted parking space contained a small bicycle rack. A Harley Davidson motorcycle was parked on one of these spacious parking lots, along with two bicycles locked to a bicycle rack.

Charlie presumed that the luxury bike had an elaborate alarm system and possibly a cut-out switch on the fuel system to eliminate an attempt of theft.

Another parking lot had two expensive-looking bicycles, heavily chained to the designated bicycle rack. Two parking lots had no motor vehicles or bicycles, but each contained an unused bike rack.

The remaining parking lot contained a bicycle and *three* scooters, covered in colourful stickers of well-known rock bands: Cheap Trick, Motley Crue, Black Sabbath, Deep Purple, and many others.

Once Charlie had moved everything from his vehicle to the inside of the unit accommodation, he immediately connected his large wide-screen television to one of the power points. A few minutes later, a jug of water was boiling.

Charlie (for the next half hour) relaxed in the comfortable lounge suite, happily sipping a cup of tea, and watching one of his favourite television programs.

Eventually, Charlie unpacked and organised the rest of his belongings, a task completed as the early evening approached. After consuming a takeaway meal, he decided to explore the building complex.

On the third level of the complex, there were four units. After Charlie had walked down the emergency fire escape stairwell, he discovered (on the second level) three more units and a spacious communal kitchen, sandwiched between two lounge areas.

Using another stairwell, he casually made his way to the ground level. This level contained four rooms, mostly used as 'meeting rooms'.

Instead of walls, each room was separated by a colourful, *Chinese restaurant-influenced* partition. This also meant that one large room could be created, simply by folding each partition and, thus, moving them along ceiling tracks towards a wall.

Over the next few days, Charlie discovered that the rooms were used for several purposeful reasons. Although they were extensively used for 'activist' meetings, other activities also occasionally took place in these rooms such as card or board game nights; furniture-making workshops; and art creativity classes – especially in designing and making colourful protest banners for regularly held street demonstrations or parades.

Located on the ground level was a small café, adjoined to a much larger-sized restaurant. The café was open between 6:00 a.m. to 3:00 p.m. each day. To dissuade older or elderly patrons, it was notoriously known for providing cardboard-padded milk crates for seating!

The restaurant was open every evening from 6:00 p.m. to 9:00 p.m. It was also open from noon to 3:00 p.m. on weekends for lunch.

Next door, there was what was commonly deemed by local inhabitants as a *retro trendy* bar. Antiquated furniture with a 'homely' appearance was messily sprawled throughout the venue. This key feature was meant to be the main attraction for the local 'hipster' crowd!

The dimly lit bar was only open from Thursday to Sunday, from 7:00 p.m. to midnight. Regarded as a 'place to chill' the bar regularly attracted a diverse ensemble of soloist musicians such as violinists, saxophonists, keyboard players – even banjo and ukulele players.

The next morning, Charlie purchased a PTC (Public Transport Covidorne) card at a 24/7 convenience store and topped up the card with fifty dollars of credit points.

A few minutes later, Charlie boarded a tram and scanned his newly purchased PTC card. It was his first-ever trip on a tram. He stood near the doorway as there was no available seating; the carriage was overcrowded – mostly with sleep-deprived and grumpy commuters.

The claustrophobic conditions of the twenty-minute tram journey along Kiddenee Road were less than ideal!

Eventually, Charlie alighted from the tram and casually strolled along a rough-surfaced footpath for about three hundred metres before arriving at the main entrance of the Prestige University.

After going through several corridors, Charlie located the main administration office. A short time later, he confirmed his enrolment by completing several paper forms.

Charlie had already completed the first several parts of the enrolment process (online) whilst still at his parent's place in

Ratatatatutra. He was now officially enrolled to undertake a four-year bachelor's degree in civil engineering!

Later, Charlie was inside a lecture hall with other first-year students. Once again, he had to complete another form, before participating in the informative but brief orientation session.

Forty-five minutes later, a mostly non-plussed Charlie was shuffling through the lecture hall towards the exit and was surrounded by a swarm of *beaming* first-year student hopefuls.

A few moments later, Charlie was walking along the rough-surfaced footpath again, heading towards a tram stop on Kiddenee Road.

After waiting for several minutes, Charlie boarded the tram once more. This time he could sit down as it was barely half full, peacefully peering through the window throughout the journey. Charlie enjoyed this tram trip far more than the first one!

Over the next three days, Charlie would eventually meet the other residents of the Spirit of Wokeness building complex. It did not take him long to realise that he was now living with quite a vibrant, diverse, and somewhat 'colourful' group of people!

2 Meet the Residents

The following morning, Charlie met one of his next-door neighbours. The solidly built and heavily tattooed gentleman, who resided in unit number five, introduced himself as *Lazer*.

As the pair conversed, Lazer soon revealed that his Christian name was Laszlo. Although born in Australia, his father was Polish-born, whilst his mother was born in the Baltic country of Estonia.

Over the next few weeks, Charlie would learn a great deal about Lazer and, similarly, with the other six residents of the building complex. Charlie soon realised that he shared a similar passion to Lazer – regular consumption of craft beers.

At the time, Lazer was employed at a microbrewery in Hiptoun; one of twenty-four in the shire of Borebland.

Outside his field of employment, Lazer's social life centred heavily around combative activities such as paintball, archery 'wars' (with plastic bows and arrows) and what could be best described as modern-day medieval combat that involved the wearing of protective clothing, war-painted faces, swords, and shields.

Throughout Borebland Shire, weekend demonstrations were a regular pastime. Some of these demonstrations tended to be nothing more than 'schoolyard battles' between activist groups over a difference of opinion!

Two groups in particular, Anarchy International and Patriots Forever, regularly clashed and would be engaged in 'planned' street warfare.

Lazer was a member of *both* groups. Charlie would soon join the Patriots Forever group. Two weeks later, however, the group disbanded, but the pair immediately joined another group: the Beef and Beer Bogan Pride Association (the new combatants for Anarchy International).

Wearing a face mask (covering the bottom part of his face), Lazer would actively be involved in these physical street encounters. He would, however, switch sides on a regular alternating basis.

This meant that Lazer would be a *frontline warrior* with Anarchy International for one week and the following week, he would do battle with the other side.

Charlie, occasionally, would assist the Beef and Beer Bogan Pride Association (BABBPA) group, especially when they were outnumbered by Anarchy International. Most of the time, however, he preferred to be just a passive onlooker. Lazer and Charlie mostly walked to these demonstrations, as they lived nearby.

When travelling to another suburb, the pair would travel together either in Charlie's 'retro-mobile' or Lazer's multi-dented Toyota Camry. The latter vehicle often reeked of stale beer and the passenger floors were completely concealed by numerous empty beer bottles and food packaging such as pizza boxes, food wrappers and styrofoam boxes!

Lazer and Charlie also discovered that they shared another common interest: hotel trivia nights. Throughout Hiptoun and other neighbouring suburbs, trivia nights were a popular and well-supported pastime by the (mostly) local inhabitants.

The pair organised a Tuesday night trivia team, one that would alternate between three different venues from week to week. Several weeks later, the team contained six regular players, having recruited other Spirit of Wokeness residents.

Charlie's other next-door neighbour (in unit seven) was Frank. Aged in his early thirties, he had been receiving disability pension payments for over ten years and passed his time away by continually enrolling as a student and spending endless hours on his personal computer.

Frank had never driven a car nor ridden a bicycle for several years. As a member of a local pro-public transport activist group, Frank used Covidorne's thriving tram system extensively. Refusing to walk more than a hundred metres at a time, Frank would only walk to one of three places: a nearby supermarket, a twenty-four-hour convenience store or the nearest tram stop. The nearest train station was five hundred metres away.

Instead of walking to the train station, Frank instead opted to first walk to the tram stop and board the next available tram. Then, at the *next* tram stop, he would alight and walk the short distance to the train station!

Frank's everyday existence centred (seemingly) around the cyber world of Internet Technology (IT). Although regarded by the other residents as an IT geek, he would still readily assist anyone who encountered problems (or faults) with their internet service or computer system.

Supplementing his disability payments, Frank regularly created websites for either individuals or small to medium-sized businesses. He was paid in cash for each completed website project.

Besides creating websites, one of Frank's 'hobbies' was hacking into business and government computer systems. He stated to Charlie and Lazer on several occasions of being previously investigated by law enforcement agencies.

Frank enjoyed his own company and the reclusive lifestyle. His unit, however, was always open for the other residents to visit and have a 'cuppa' (coffee or tea) with him anytime.

Frank was mostly a teetotaller and was renowned for not leaving his unit for days or even for a week or two, especially when creating and designing a website.

The other residents, meanwhile, suspected that Frank was more than likely trying to continuously improve and hone his hacking skills!

The occupant of unit eight was Maureen who was aged in her mid-twenties.

Charlie soon learnt that she had given herself the moniker 'Moo' many years earlier, largely in defiance of being referred to as *Mo* by her family, a name she utterly detested. Moo's much-valued possession was a Harley Davidson motorcycle, given to her as a twenty-first birthday present.

Both Moo's parents had belonged to a Harley Davidson Club. She parked her motorcycle in one of the underground parking lots, along with two bicycles (locked to a bike rack) which she rarely ever rode.

Moo and Lazer had known each other for several years and were currently part-time lovers. They both opposed the idea of being committed to a serious full-time relationship. Charlie also learnt that Moo was bisexual and would occasionally engage in sexual activity with one of the other Spirit of Wokeness residents (Angelica).

Despite being an 'eternal-studying' art student, Moo was nevertheless able to regularly earn a comfortable income by selling numerous artworks at various venues whether it be inside a friend's art gallery, in several cafes (including the ground-level café and bar inside the building complex) and at weekend markets located within the Borebland shire.

As an enthusiastic supporter of the regular street protests throughout Borebland Shire, Moo often accompanied Lazer and her fellow art students to what was entertainingly referred to as *peaceful gatherings*.

These somewhat 'peaceful gatherings' were quite colourful spectacles, further enhanced by numerous artistically creative banners and posters, proudly held high by enthusiastic protesters.

Moo was part of a uniquely creative team that used their artistic skills to design and create these eye-catching protest banners and posters.

Many of these banners and posters were created at the *University of Woke and Knowledge* where Moo was undertaking yet another Arts Degree. However, some banners and posters were created in one of the several meeting/activity rooms in the Spirit of Wokeness complex.

Street artwork, including the walls of several buildings, provided another source of income for Moo. She regularly created colourful designs or patterns on pavements outside diverse types of businesses such as cafes, bars, vinyl record shops and bookshops.

Moo's favourite artwork accomplishments, however, were her creation of unique-styled graffiti-like murals on the sides or the fronts of several types of buildings such as the local craft breweries, art galleries, hobby centres and retro clothing warehouses.

The occupant of unit four (on the third level) was Alek. Aged in his mid-thirties, he was a friendly character who presented an outwardly vibrant and flamboyant personality.

Alek was well known and liked throughout the Borebland shire.

Alek's calm and outgoing demeanour was also well received by the residents in the building complex. He was one of those somewhat stereotypical individuals who seemingly had no enemies.

Employed part-time in a cheese-making factory located in Hiptoun, Alek was best known as a popular trivia host within the local area, particularly in the suburbs of Hiptoun and Bunnslich. He even had his own trivia company, *Smart Alek Trivia Co.* Alek hosted hotel trivia nights, three to five nights per week.

A huge fan of the 1970s and 1980s rock bands, the walls of his unit were covered with numerous band posters. In the Spirit of Wokeness's underground parking lot, Alek had a bicycle and three scooters: a motorcycle scooter; a fold-up kick scooter; and a child's non-electric scooter.

Idolising his favourite rock bands, all four modes of transport were covered with numerous rock album stickers: Cheap Trick, Black Sabbath, and Deep Purple – just to name a few.

Alek rarely used public transport. Inside his unit, there were several pairs of roller skates. Each pair of skates had what could be best described as having flashing 'disco-styled' lights. Every weekend, he would *blissfully* skate inside the Bunnslich roller-skating rink for several hours.

Another key interest of Alek's involvement within the entertainment industry was in the field of improvised comedy.

Every Sunday evening, he was either a performer with the Impro of Covidorne Theatre Company or just a mere humble member of the audience.

The company was based in the suburb of Piranha (several suburbs away from Hiptoun) and owned a spacious studio that contained the following: a sizeable stage; seating for three hundred people; and a small canteen that sold an assortment of snack food, along with hot and cold beverages that were also non-alcoholic.

Many of the improvised theatre performers had appeared in numerous television commercials advertising such items as shampoos, toothpaste, and beard-trimming products.

Several of the impro-comedy actors had also previously featured in a series of health insurance commercials.

Several years earlier, Alek had even been employed as a 'hipster' fashion model and was part of a short-lived television production named *Men's Innovative Fashion Today.*

The other residents resided in the three remaining units (third level) of the Spirit of Wokeness building complex.

Angelica occupied unit number three. She was currently employed as a community liaison officer and had been a student at the University of Woke and Knowledge.

Angelica had attained several degrees and diplomas over many years in several learning areas such as woke politics, gender-neutral studies, marginalised community agendas and progressive education methods.

When Charlie first encountered Angelica, her eye-catching luminescent rainbow-coloured hairstyle instantly 'leapt out' at him!

Angelica's hair had been dyed with six separate colours, blatantly representing her personalised patriotic tribute to the local LGBTQ social acceptance movement.

After being involved with a string of LGBTQ movements over several years, she was the president (and a former co-founder) of the alternative lifestyle group, the FEMCJDON+ community. It was a splinter group to the long-established LGBTQAHIKP+ community.

Angelica's long-term and overly-passionate support of the several locally marginalised communal groups had earned her a respected status of being regarded as a somewhat legendary icon within the Borebland region.

Similarly to most of the Shire's residents, Angelica was also an active participant in Borebland's ever-thriving fringe political movements.

Angelica regularly participated in street protest marches and as a *frontline performer*, typically characterised by carrying a protest banner in one hand and a loud hailer in the other. Her booming and articulate voice was a source of inspiration to other like-minded protesters!

In the underground parking lot, Angelica's parking space was vacant. She was a regular user of Covidorne's efficient public transport system. Train and tram services especially.

Angelica rarely used bus services and like Frank, she had never had a driver's licence. Two or three times per week, though, Angelica would be transported from one place to another as a passenger in a small vehicle driven by her friend and fellow Spirit of Wokeness resident, Hazelle.

Unit number two was occupied by another of Angelica's close friends: Florence. Aged in her late twenties and better known as Floozie, she was born and raised in what could be best described as a 'wilderness commune' on the island of Diemania. The northernmost point of the island was nearly six hundred kilometres from the southern tip of the state of Luzerstan.

Courtesy of a journey on a simply constructed seaworthy vessel made from locally-produced timber, Floozie 'migrated' from the relatively primitive Diemanian port of Hobotart to Covidorne's main ferry port, Port Covidorne, just after her twentieth birthday.

A diehard cycling enthusiast, Floozie owned two bicycles. When not in use, both were heavily chained to a bike rack in her designated parking space.

Floozie's main bicycle was either used for cycling within the Borebland Shire or the occasional bicycle trip to and from other areas within Covidorne. She too had never had a driver's licence, largely because of her fiercely staunch and somewhat fanatical stance of being opposed to petrol-driven or diesel-driven motor vehicles.

Floozie, however, did approve the use of electric vehicles (not hybrid ones though) albeit with certain 'limitations'. She would only walk to venues or retail outlets that were located close to the residential complex. Floozie rarely used public transport.

Floozie's second bicycle, an endurance road bike (costing just over $3,500), was solely used for long-distance cycling. Throughout the year, she would regularly cycle with a group of cyclists, mostly for distances of at least fifty kilometres and on the weekends.

Several times a year, Floozie would cycle for hundreds of kilometres. She was also an ardent member of *three* local cycling gangs: Extinction Rebels, Bicycle Lycra Matters and Cyclists of the Earth.

Away from Floozie's passion for cycling, her favourite pastimes evolve around frequent participation in various activist meetings and her local church group: the Born-Again Vegan Ministry.

A mass service was held in the Born-Again Vegan church every morning, but it would be the Sunday (morning) mass that was quite popular. Several hundred avid parishioners attended this regular service. Each one-hour service of 'holy redemption' was conducted by one of three Gaia priestesses wearing robes consisting of just one colour – green.

A monumental feature of the Born-Again Vegan Ministry was to highlight the welfare of a particular animal each week.

The sermon, charismatically (and hysterically) delivered by a Gaia priestess, focused deeply on this concept. The term *meat is murder* was regularly uttered throughout each sermon.

After the Sunday morning service had ended, parishioners were then treated to a feast of vegan-friendly plant-based food and beverages.

The weekly Sunday event was largely deemed as a 'meet and greet' session and donations of gold coins and notes were generously appreciated. Overzealous parishioners, quite theatrically, would drop gold coins *slowly* into the donation box and, in turn, eye off the not-so-generous ones!

Next door to Floozie, in unit one, resided a woman in her mid-thirties: Hazelle. Like Floozie, she was employed in the state education sector.

In recent years, Hazelle had mostly been employed within Luzerstan's state education department, fulfilling several roles: teaching, administration duties, syllabus writing and as an education coordinator.

Before entering the workforce, she had been a long-term student, completing three bachelor's degrees in education, arts, and socialist politics.

Outside the education sector, one of Hazelle's key passions centred around various aspects of the art world, from painting murals to different forms of street art or to just blissfully being engaged in painting/sketching within her unit.

Every second Wednesday, she conducted street art or mural art classes inside the multi-activity room of the Spirit of Wokeness building complex.

Pink was undeniably Hazelle's favourite colour. In the underground car park, she owned a small four-cylinder and shiny, pink-coloured Volkswagen Polo. The interior was mostly pink-coloured: from the car seat covers to the dashboard console and even the steering wheel cover!

With pink streaks running through her long flowing light brown hair, Hazelle regularly wore predominately pink-coloured clothing whether it be dresses or shirts/tops – and even pink tracksuits.

Despite the obvious obsession, not all of Hazelle's clothing was pink in colour as she sometimes wore a pair of blue or black jeans, particularly in cooler weather. Her handbag and several other personal items, though, were mostly pink.

The 'interior decorating' of Hazelle's one-bedroom unit, however, could be best described as quite a *bizarre pilgrimage* to the colour pink. From the lounge suite to curtains and drapes – even tablecloths and tea towels. Equally amusing, her black-coloured cat was named Mr Pink!

As previously indicated, Angelica and Floozie were not only Hazelle's neighbours but the three of them were also close friends.

They regularly shared food (large pizzas and other takeaway meals for example) and alcoholic or non-alcoholic beverages in each other's unit. The trio also met up inside the café or the trendy 'retro' bar located within the Spirit of Wokeness building complex at least twice a week.

Hazelle was also part of Charlie's Thursday night trivia team along with Floozie, Angelica and Lazer. The trivia group alternated between two venues, both located in the neighbouring suburb of Bunnslich. She was also part of a second trivia group that divided into two or three teams on Tuesday nights. Charlie was also part of this trivia group.

Every Sunday afternoon, Hazelle was part of another group (with several of her work colleagues) that participated in a trivia event in the undercover beer garden of a South Duffel hotel. Occasionally, Angelica and Floozie would also join this group.

Charlie, meanwhile, was looking forward to his new life as a full-time student and three days later, he attended an obligatory orientation session from 9:00 a.m. to 4:00 p.m.

It was mainly conducted in a large lecture hall of Prestige University. For two hours (between midday and 2:00 p.m.), though, components of the orientation session were held outside in the picturesque garden-themed courtyard.

3   The Cultural Awakening

Hiptoun was nestled between the neighbouring suburbs of South Duffel, Barfton, Nobberk, Ritzsoy and Bunnslich; all under the central authority of the Borebland Shire Council.

In the centre of Hiptoun and on Lowe Street (the suburb's other main thoroughfare), the historical town hall building was a prominent feature of the local landscape. On top of this unique and eye-catching structure was a neon sign: 'Welcome to Hiptoun – the Suburb of Cultural Awakening.'

With a long and treasured history, the multi-roomed town hall was a hub for several social purposes: general community meetings; social functions; art exhibitions; computer swap meets; Muay Thai kickboxing events; and public speaking forums.

There were various forms of print media circulated throughout the Borebland Shire. The daily *Borebland Pravda* was the most popular one though. The newspaper, generally, only focused on local issues and events.

The Borebland Pravda typically contained the following: the main local news stories; real estate advertisements; a classified section and entertainment pages covering upcoming music gigs; poetry reading sessions; and even trivia nights. But there was one notable omission – sport.

Editors, both present and past, had refused to cover any sporting activity. Even local sporting events.

The shire of Borebland had an extensive public transport system: train stations, bus routes and tram options. Cycling, however, was the main form of transport and the extensive bicycle path system was certainly well-used.

Additionally, bicycle lanes were a key component of all the main thoroughfares throughout the shire. Due to a spate of well-supported and aggressive local activist measures, many of the streets were car-free, particularly in areas of moderate to high retail activity.

Some sections of Kiddenee Road and Lowe Street were only accessible to trams, cyclists, and pedestrians. Motorists could only use the 'car-friendly' streets that either ran parallel or perpendicular to Hiptoun's two main thoroughfares.

On weekday mornings and afternoons, many cyclists used the bicycle paths and the street bicycle lanes, supposedly riding within the white lines. Most of them were travelling to and from their place of employment.

During the peak morning and afternoon travel times, the Borebland Shire Council enforced legislation that effectively prohibited any motorised vehicles (cars, motorcycles, trucks, delivery vans, etc.) from using certain thoroughfares between the times of 6:00 a.m. to 9:00 a.m. and 4:00 p.m. to 7:00 p.m.

Charlie, meanwhile, had developed an intolerable level of disdain towards the progress of his engineering course at

Prestige University. Unfortunately, he felt that the social vibe throughout the educational facility was negative and had become quite robotic.

By the end of the fifth week, Charlie was experiencing a major sense of discontentment with his course of study, further enhanced by an overall lack of positive social discourse among students and even with the lecturers (and tutors).

After having discussions with other Spirit of Wokeness residents (Frank in particular), Charlie chose to drop out of his engineering course and disassociate himself from Prestige University altogether.

By now, Charlie had been working part-time for the past three weeks in one of the local micro-breweries with Lazer and was no longer keen to pursue any other study options for at least the next couple of weeks or so.

Charlie, though, enrolled in a new course at the University of Woke and Knowledge (in Bunnslich) four weeks later. He commenced a bachelor's degree in information technology, majoring in Business Information Systems. Charlie decided on this option, knowing that Frank would be able to provide him with a high level of assistance throughout the entire course if required.

The bachelor's degree also included many other optional certificates. By the time Charlie had finished his degree (three and a half years later), he had gained several non-information technology certificates such as advanced beer-making skills, protest banner designing and continental cheese making.

Two years before Charlie's enrolment, the University of Woke and Knowledge had acquired a global status rating of *par excellence.*

This international recognition largely resulted from the 'unique' degree courses that the educational facility offered. It focused on a diverse range of topical issues such as advanced victimhood studies, vegan dominance, snowflake politics and the lifestyles of gender-neutral hipsters!

Charlie immediately developed friendships or 'amicable associations' with many of his fellow students which, in turn, soon saw him exploring numerous aspects of Borebland's unique and diverse sub-cultures.

Over the next three or so years, he would term these new-found 'personal growth' experiences as his *cultural awakening.*

Although the city of Covidorne was renowned for its abnormally wide range of food and beverage options, compared with other major cities throughout the country of Austrutopia, the Borebland Shire had noticeably taken this concept quite a few steps further!

The proportion of microbreweries and coffee shops/cafes compared to the general population was one of the highest in the country; particularly in Hiptoun and Bunnslich.

The 'effervescent' coffee culture had long established a reputation for being *flamboyantly creative.* Soya-based lattes, in particular, had long been a favourite beverage amongst the local population for quite some time.

Coffee boutiques and cafes regularly competed against each other, creating an array of outlandish or artistic coffee alternatives such as turmeric lattes, charcoal/Goth coffees, unicorn cappuccinos, and many other exotic styles of coffee.

Food cuisine in the Borebland shire was also regarded as 'flamboyantly unique'. Items like tofu, kale, kimchi, smashed avocado, and *vegan delights* were prominent on the menus of all eating places.

Surprisingly, though, one food item surpassed them all – pizza. The pizza culture scene was even more competitive and, in turn, inexpensive for the average customer.

From gourmet pizzas to even the standard ones, there appeared to be no limit to what toppings enthusiastic pizza-making chefs or cooks would use in an attempt to create the ultimate pizza-dining experience for their customers.

Pizzas would also be one of Charlie's favourite meals over the next several years and he would typically devour at least three of them each week. From souvlaki-influenced pizzas to seafood-dominated ones – Charlie enjoyed them all. Even the bizarre ones such as prawn and salami combination pizzas to the ones where tofu, pumpkin, beetroot, feta, and kale were 'harmoniously combined' to create a pizza masterpiece!

Among the numerous eateries and hotels/bars, other small businesses were also in plentiful supply such as vinyl record stores, tattoo parlours, musical instrument retail outlets, retro clothing retailers and art studios.

To further enhance his culture-awakening experiences, Charlie also joined several social activist groups and was a regular attendee at various meeting events. Some of these formal gatherings were organised and held in one of the conference rooms of the Spirit of Wokeness building complex.

Another significant aspect of Charlie's thriving social lifestyle involved his active participation in street rallies (or demonstrations) within the Borebland shire, particularly the ones in Hiptoun and Bunnslich.

4 A Feast of Festivals, Contests and Tours

Throughout the Borebland Shire, *a feast of festivals, contests and tours* contributed significantly to the thriving social scene.

The suburb of Hiptoun was regarded as the centrepiece for these events of vast extravaganza and 'progressive' moments of cultural uplifting.

Various festivals took place throughout Borebland each month, consisting of a high degree of colourful flamboyancy and clamorous noise. Despite a few festivals being held solely on an annual basis, most were recurring ones, typically taking place five or six times per year.

A notable exception, however, was the *Hippy Flippy Culture Extravaganza*, held on the first Sunday of each calendar month. This event enthusiastically attempted to celebrate all aspects, irrespective of any given degree of relevance, of an ever-thriving Borebland hipster sub-culture.

On the first Sunday of January of each year, *digital attendance passports* were issued to the over-excitable attendees of the first Hippy Flippy Culture Extravaganza for the year.

These passports would be filled with event participation stamps at each monthly event. In return, recipients would then be gifted with the highly sought-after digital coupons and vouchers, provided by numerous local (mainly) sponsors.

These coupons and vouchers would, thus, enable the event-participating individual to gain access to a wide range of promotional products: free glasses of locally crafted beer; free mugs of soy-based coffee lattes; free 'exotic' pizzas; and even the occasional food hamper, successfully acquired once an attendee had accumulated a certain number of participation stamps or a minimum number of coupons.

The standard food hamper contained the following: a variety of continental cheeses; multi-flavoured blocks of tofu; falafel balls; containers of kimchi, alfalfa sprouts and kale; non-plastic packets of chia seeds; and fresh quinoa plants.

The general festival format consisted of three key aspects: the colourful and flamboyant street parade; numerous stalls (side by side) lined along the street; and sit-down eateries, overflowing with exuberant patronage. The small cafes and restaurants, however, blatantly flouted the Luzerstan's state regulations concerning seating capacity limits.

Comfortable medium-sized chairs were often replaced with milk crates or narrow high stools. This meant that instead of having six chairs placed around a table, ten to twelve milk crates (for example) surrounded the table, mirroring sardine-like seating arrangements.

The faithful patrons, mostly millennials and those within the Generation Z age bracket, sat next to each other, shoulder to shoulder – even when eating a meal. The recommended *social distancing* directives by the Borebland Shire Council were largely ignored!

Within these small-sized eateries, table spacing required a certain amount of improvisation. A few eateries had some tables of equal size, but most venues had ones of varying shapes and sizes.

The arrangement of the tables and chairs was strategically designed to squeeze in as many patrons as possible. This now meant that there was minimal space between tables or groups of people, thus, severely limiting manoeuvrable movement for patrons. One wonders whether Tetris-playing geniuses were specifically hired to ensure maximum seating capacity!

As the conditions were ridiculously cramped at times, a certain number of patrons found themselves alternating between standing and sitting in their 'prized' dining spot, just so that other patrons could move in and out of their dining space. Then there were the *windowsill* tables.

Many of the eateries had windowsills, just big enough to fit one or two small to medium-sized plates (or bowls) on them. High narrow stools were the only type of seating used at these windowsill tables.

At full capacity, patrons were seated shoulder to shoulder along these narrow windowsills. Once again, arm movements were quite limited for those trying to eat a meal.

The monthly Hippy Flippy Culture Extravaganza saw a healthy array of activities. Firstly, there was the ever-popular *bearded flower and garden* contest where artistically minded contestants weaved, platted, or styled their hirsute facial growth into miniature woven baskets of various shapes!

Flowers were strategically intertwined with the numerous hair fibres, creating what became known as a *beard bouquet*.

There were several other beard-growing contests as well. The most popular one was the bearded celebrity-lookalike where the goal for participants was to match the nominated bearded celebrity (or historical character) for a particular month.

Examples included Ned Kelly, ZZ Top (except for the drummer who had the ironic name of Frank Beard), Karl Marx, Charles Darwin, Santa Claus (where contestants were required to dye their beards white) and Hans Langseth (who?).

For the males (or non-gender specific individuals) who were not as fortunate to be 'hirsute-gifted' a similar contest was held: the *man-bun flower and garden* contest.

Like the bearded flower and garden contest, the various participants used their man-buns to create an artistically creative and unique hair floral arrangement.

In both contests, judges presented ribbons to the top three participants. All contestants, however, received gifts (e.g. a six-pack of locally crafted bottled beer), keeping in line with the traditional local sub-cultural belief that 'everyone is a winner'.

The concept of 'winners and losers' within the Borebland shire was generally deemed as being discriminatory.

Held every second month, the *Everything Vegan* parade and festival was also a popular drawcard; even attracting people who resided outside the Borebland Shire. The January festival parade was heavily advertised and widely promoted throughout Austrutopia.

Vegan alternative life-stylers travelled long distances from cities, towns and what could be best described as 'alternative settlements' within Luzerstan and other states as well. Even families from the oft-forgotten state of Leperwest journeyed for several days before reaching the Borebland shire.

The *Everything Vegan* parade took place in Hiptoun, along a three-hundred-metre stretch on Kiddenee Road. Parade floats led the festive parade.

Following these flamboyantly decorative and uniquely artistic float platforms, placard-waving vegan devotees proudly marched with an obvious diminutive purpose.

At the forefront of the group, the Borebland Green Gaia Mayor (and national president of the Vegan Activist Society) carried a large loudhailer, leading the faithful masses in a noisy repetitive recital of several well-known mantras such as *veganism is always number one.*

Family groups, often led by over-smiling and starry-eyed children, made up at least a third of the marching group. But humans were not the only participants. Many 'vegan canines' also intermingled freely with the scores of spectators.

These adorable pooches even wore coats of advertising or promotional slogans.

A white Labrador dog, for example, wore a sign stating: 'Hi, my name is Tofu. My favourite foods are soybeans, pinto beans, lentils, rice, oats, and sweet potatoes!'

Once the parade was completed, typically between midday and 12:30 p.m., participants and onlookers made their way to a large recreational area. They were instantly greeted with several rows of food and non-food tent stalls. Before setting up a food stall, however, the stallholder was required to obtain a permit.

Several *vegan food compliance officers*, easily recognised by their all-green clothing (with red, white, and black insignia on both upper sleeves), inspected ALL food items ensuring they were strictly plant-based vegan products. Once satisfied, the stallholder was granted the required permit to operate for the rest of the day.

Another popular festival event was the three-day Mardi Gras (held twice a year) that popularised the alternative lifestyle communities.

The first Mardi Gras was held in June, coinciding with a national long weekend holiday. It commenced at noon on a Saturday and finished late afternoon on Monday.

The second Mardi Gras was held in the last week of October, coinciding with a state-wide holiday. It commenced at noon on Friday and finished well into the evening on Sunday. The formats for both festival events were similar.

Both Mardi Gras began with a street march parade, led by the LGBTQAHIKP+ community. Behind the several flag-bearers (each carrying a large rainbow-themed one), artistic and colourful placards dominated the overall street marching vibe. The next group of marchers was the FEMCJDON+ community: a splinter group from the LGBTQAHIKP+.

This group consisted of biological females, transgender females or even those that identified themselves as being 'female-oriented'.

Whilst many of their ideals were like the main group, they were primarily different in the sense that they passionately believed that females should always come first − especially when engaging in any form of sexual activity.

Most of this group also belonged to another prominent Borebland community group: the Witchy Bitches Femo Club (WBFC).

Angelica (president and a co-founder of FEMCJDON+) proudly led the group, holding a banner depicting a red-coloured silhouette of a female standing with one foot on the head of a blue-coloured silhouette of a male who is lying down in a hapless position! The depicted female punches the air with a raised fist, supposedly symbolising a 'victory of defiance'.

The background of the flag is fluorescent pink with bright, purple-coloured borders.

Before the commencement of the street parade at noon, food and beverage stalls (lined closely together near the footpath) had been set up within the previous two hours. Cafes had already opened their doors several hours earlier.

Attendees, many still hungover from the previous night's social activities, soon filled the cafes and sought suitable food or drink 'remedies' from the newly set-up stalls.

The street-march parade lasted for just over an hour and was essentially an exercise in 'meeting and greeting' the attendees. The main street parade would be held later in the evening.

The LGBTQAHIKP+ and FEMCJDON+ communities (along with several smaller communities) would transform themselves from bohemian-influenced or retro-influenced dressed members into ones that were now elegantly garbed in decoratively flamboyant costumes of extreme glamour and glitz for the main evening street parade.

Just after 12:30 p.m., nine mobile kitchens were set up in the middle of the street. The *cuisine contests* soon commenced and were held throughout the three-day festival. Local chefs, cooks, baristas, and brewers, representing various Borebland businesses, would put their skills to the test, promoting and advertising their unique style of food and beverage products.

As with other festival contests, the concept of *everyone's a winner* was still applied and, subsequently, every contestant would be gifted a prize.

The nine mobile kitchens were categorised and set up as follows:

1. Exotic vegan delights (the first mobile kitchen).

2. Best smashed avocado presentation

3. Quirkiest coffee top-layer design.

4. Floral sprinkling designs on various food dishes.

5. Most unique cooking style of 'sunny side' eggs.

6. Most flamboyant ethereal ice cream.

7. Freakshakes and deconstructed coffee.

8. Craft beers (ales, lagers, and stouts).

9. Best barbequed red meat and craft beer combinations (the last mobile kitchen).

Due to previous indifferences and hostile disagreements that resulted in the occasional scuffle or skirmish, pro-meat supporters and anti-meat vegan devotees were kept away from each other as much as possible. Hence, the deliberate positioning of the first mobile kitchen and the last one!

The *colourful* and *decibel-defying* Mardi Gras Street festival commenced at 6:00 p.m. A few minutes after 8:00 p.m., a temporary stage was set up. The 'Battle of the local Indie and Alternative Bands' would begin just after 9:00 p.m.

The first Indie artists were the ones that were making their public debuts, a monumental step up from performing in space-limited unit lounge rooms or jamming in parental-owned house basements!

On Sunday night, the *Battle of the local Indie and Alternative Bands* featured acts that had performed regularly (or semi-regularly) for at least twelve months. Each band played for about fifteen minutes.

Some of these bands had attracted a regular group of people to past hotel or restaurant performances and, thus, had what could be best described as having a 'niche audience' following.

On the third (and final) day of the Mardi Gras, several well-known and popular local indie bands performed together throughout the late afternoon. This penultimate event of the three-day festival morphed into the final street-march parade.

The exuberant participants, who were the same people in the opening parade of day one, farewelled the Mardi Gras attendees amidst a frantic volume of noisy fanfare and over-enthusiastic handwaving.

Throughout the festival, the ever-popular microbrewery tours also took place. Bookings were essential for each event, despite microbreweries conducting tours regularly during any week, especially on the weekends, throughout the year.

A distinguishing feature of these tours was that they were mostly organised and hosted by self-acclaimed *hipsters* who typically sported well-grown beards, man-buns, and tattoos.

A notable exception, however, was Lazer. Although he had numerous tattoos, his scraggy-like beard and unique hairstyle (a mohawk style with dreadlocks) certainly stood out when he assisted in conducting tours at the microbrewery where he was employed!

5 The Sunday Protests

A tradition that had begun over twenty years ago, the *Sunday Protests* was a distinct cultural and iconic event, synonymous with the 'woke warfare' within Borebland Shire.

The suburb of Hiptoun was the centrepiece as most street protests took place along Kiddenee Road each Sunday. Occasionally, street protests took place in the neighbouring suburbs of South Duffel or Bunnslich as well, but only if two or more street parade festivals occurred simultaneously.

The procedure for the street protests contained the same protocols each Sunday. Large crowds were allowed to line the street blocks of Kiddenee Road from 11:00 a.m. Before this time, large portable bollards had been placed to deny any pedestrian access to the public.

Heavyset security personnel, many of them sporting man-buns and Ned Kelly-like beards, from the Pinkerton Mob (one of the more prominent bicycle gangs in the Borebland shire) 'policed' the area and ensured the bollards remained in place until 11:00 a.m.

Just before the commencement of The Sunday Protests at noon, tram services ceased to operate. Access for any type of motor vehicle or recreational cyclist had already been halted since 9:00 a.m.

Widely advertised and promoted as a 'tourist event', the first protest group began marching from noon.

Although many street-marching participants were affiliated with multiple protest causes, several groups focused primarily on woke information and awareness campaigns, handing out leaflets to spectators lined along the edge of the road.

These awareness campaigns were intrinsically linked with key issues such as global warming/climate change, animal extinction movements and anti-coal activism – just to name a few.

As the protestors and awareness campaigners made their way along Kiddenee Road, they were joined by a large group of protesting cyclists, many of whom were associated with one of the localised bicycle gangs.

Whilst the intent of the street protest mainly centred on sending out subliminal messages in quite an aggressive and provocative manner, the weekly event was still greeted with a carnival-like atmosphere.

Colourful banners and placards, intertwined with a unified aura of personality vivaciousness, further enhanced with gaudy but eye-catching clothing attire, dominated the general visual scene.

It was quite a spectacle for the well-wishing attendees lined (shoulder-to-shoulder) along the footpaths of Hiptoun's main street. Then there was the excitable clamour of noise!

Among the hysterical yelling, screaming, and chanting (or call it what you like), an array of music styles soon added an electrified vibe to the overall street extravaganza.

A large group of taiko drummers was strategically placed between large lobbying groups. Their role seemed to be one of 'support' where quick sets of rapid drumming filled the void between the bouts of hysterical and repetitive chanting.

Most of the devoted lobbyists used this pause time to chat idly amongst themselves. They also used this opportunity to take large sips of a liquid replenishment to rejuvenate hoarse vocal cords!

The over-enthusiastic taiko drummers, however, were not the only aspiring musicians strategically dispersed amongst the street protestors and woke awareness campaigners.

Marching band drummers (snare, tenor, and the occasional bass) and cymbalists were placed between the smaller groups of protestors.

The local ukulele club played their instruments in an uncanny but coordinated manner, whilst at the tail of the carnival-like protesting spectacle, there was an *unusual* group of musicians.

Some of these musicians played what may be best described as 'medieval' instruments. Others tried to eke out a tune by banging metal rods against pots or pans!

Along with the directionless clanger of unmelodic noise, the other key factor that attracted the attention of the average street attendee was the markedly 'unorthodox' dress sense.

Words like bohemian (or boho), vintaged, retro-styled, and 'pre-loved' generally dominated the overall fashion spectacle, clearly demonstrated by the enthusiastic groups of protesting awareness campaigners and even amongst a sizeable portion of the gathered crowd of onlookers as well.

Throughout Borebland, boutique clothing outlets were plentiful. Home-made clothing (and clothing accessories) was quite a popular pastime, particularly among the younger generations and even the 'young-at-heart' who were mostly females.

The large and renowned retail clothing companies were largely shunned by the 'hipster-influenced' residents. Austrutopian and international clothing retail chains were no longer in existence throughout Borebland Shire.

A history of low turnover sales had prompted these retail giants to close their stores and, thus, relocate to suburbs where their businesses would likely be more profitable.

Security for the Sunday Protests was provided by one of the most prominent (and largely feared) local bicycle gangs: the notorious Pinkerton Mob. Clad in pink Lycra from neck to toe, their main task was to deal with 'unruly and offensive' dissidents who dared to upset the positive and flowing vibe demonstrated throughout the day's events. They lined both sides of Kiddenee Road during the street protest procession to ensure suitable space for the marching participants and, thus, clearly separating them from the onlookers.

The Pinkerton Mob's mostly black-coloured bicycles were partially covered in temporary blue and white police masking tape. A large flashing red and blue light was attached to the middle of the handlebars, along with a bullhorn and a siren which sounded uncannily like one used during a wartime air raid!

The weekly Sunday Protest would conclude between 2:00 p.m. and 3:00 p.m. Just past the intersection of Kiddenee Road and Wokespark Avenue, the protesting and campaigning participants would enter the Ironic Icon Park Reserve.

Numerous food stalls and several beverage stalls were already set up. As the protestors passed through the arched entrance, they were provided with free tofu, avocado bread rolls and a recyclable bottle of local-made ginger beer.

Once all the protesting participants had entered the park reserve, the public was allowed to enter (through the arched entrance) and into the perimeter-fenced designated area as directed by the burly and surly members of the Pinkerton Mob.

6   Beware of the Cyclists

Hiptoun was renowned throughout the city of Covidorne as a centrepiece for a variety of sub-culture uniqueness due to a diverse range of reasons that included the following: the regular street parades; marches and protests; clusters of diverse community groups; vegan religious church services; retro vinyl records outlets; the second-hand book stores; being a vibrant hub for the numerous works of graffiti street art and art galleries; the University of Woke and Knowledge; the numerous micro-breweries and an abnormally high ratio of cafes or coffee shops in comparison to the number of local inhabitants. And then there were the militant bicycle gangs!

Outside the shire of Borebland, the 'media collective' often described these militant bicycle gangs as the *bicycle mafia.*

The key operations were based in Hiptoun, but the 'bicycle mafia' also owned numerous building complexes throughout Borebland Shire that contained microbreweries, cafes/coffee shops and restaurants, bicycle storage facilities and bicycle repair shops. These buildings were colloquially known as *clubhouses.*

Over many years, persistent rumours were rife of a 'secret' (and tightly secured) room within many of these clubhouses, which was supposedly used for the production of well-known illicit substances!

Eight bicycle gangs, easily identifiable by their specific Lycra colours, were based in Borebland Shire:

- Pinkerton Mob (pink Lycra)
- Lycra Mongrols (dark brown Lycra)
- Commanding Daredevils (black and yellow Lycra)
- Extinction Rebels (red Lycra)
- Rainbow Ruffians (rainbow-coloured Lycra)
- Green Forever Squad (grass-green coloured Lycra)
- Bicycle Lycra Matters (black, white, and red Lycra)
- Cyclists of the Earth (fluorescent green and red Lycra)

Over the years, the 'bicycle mafia' has played a significant role in infiltrating and influencing numerous decision-making processes conducted within the Borebland Shire Council.

A popular rumour in circulation insinuated that the current Green Gaia Mayor (along with several other council members) enjoyed close links to senior hierarchical members of several cycling gangs; namely the Pinkerton Mob, the Extinction Rebels, and the Lycra Mongrols.

The council was renowned for deciding on numerous favourable outcomes to appease the unified demands of the eight cycling gangs.

Previous Borebland Shire councils had cemented quite a firm reputation within Covidorne as being largely friendless towards any motorised vehicles – cars in particular.

A long history of persistent and aggravated hostilities by militant bicycle gangs led to motor vehicles either being banned in some streets or only permitted to travel within a set time limit in certain areas of Borebland shire, notably within the central business districts and subsequent nearby streets or laneways.

Whilst bicycle repair (or modification) services and sales flourished throughout Borebland, motor vehicle dealers and mechanical repairers were now nowhere to be seen. Previous unsavoury incidents between motor vehicle dealers (along with mechanics) and the bicycle gangs eventually saw the latter emerge victorious. As a result, a motorised vehicle could only be purchased, repaired, serviced, or modified outside the boundaries of the Borebland Shire!

Militant cycling lobbyists had previously resorted to blatant acts of extreme terrorist activity in an endeavour to achieve their desired outcomes.

Notable examples of this extreme terrorist activity being inflicted upon motor vehicle dealers and mechanical repairers included the following: the sporadic firebombing and graffiti attacks of car dealerships/vehicle repairer workshops; threats of personal safety to owners/franchisees and their employees; bizarre rules and regulations ruthlessly implemented upon the owners and franchisees by the Borebland Shire council; and, an ever-consistent campaign of cyber-attacks and cyber-bullying, largely through regular attempts of hacking into the websites of these types of businesses, particularly via the use of denial-of-service (DoS) attacks.

Proprietors of bicycle sales outlets, along with cycling repair businesses as well, regularly placed themselves at the forefront of any anti-motor vehicle campaigns within the major suburbs of the Borebland Shire.

These anti-motor vehicle campaigns also involved hard-hitting signage on building walls and windows that included:

1. Cars are not welcome in Hiptoun.
2. Motor vehicles damage the environment.
3. Vehicle drivers - enter the area at your OWN risk.
4. Cars will have their wheels chopped off.

As aforementioned, bicycle repair shops were often part of a bicycle gang clubhouse. Several cycling retail outlets also doubled up as clubhouses, particularly when used as a meeting place. Well-planned and militant-styled courses of action or successful lobbying campaigns had their origins within the walls of these buildings.

Within Covidorne, the bizarre road rules imposed by the Borebland Shire council, legislated for both cyclists and non-cyclists, were widely regarded by 'outsiders' (anyone living outside of Borebland) as being quite cringeworthy.

The foremost and simplest road rule for everyone to follow within the Borebland area, however, was that motor vehicles were *always* required to give way to cyclists.

Whilst cyclists were able to enjoy the luxury of not having to adhere to any speed limits, motorised vehicles (cars, trucks, motorbikes and even mopeds/scooters) were only permitted to travel at a maximum speed of thirty kilometres per hour along most of the streets within the shire. Many of the streets and laneways contained speed humps but cycling paths/lanes were speedhump-free!

A little-known group of enthusiasts, the *Friendly Society of Moped and Scooter Riders*, had previously attempted to lobby the Borebland Shire council (on three separate occasions) to be granted the same road-use rights as cyclists. Alas, they were unsuccessful. This was primarily due to the cycling gangs successfully infiltrating and influencing the council's decision-making process on each of these three occasions.

Roller skaters and users of non-motorised scooters, on the other hand, were slightly more successful in lobbying the Borebland Shire council to be granted at least some of the cycling road-use rights, but they were still only granted a small number of concessions.

As with motorists or motorbike riders, roller skaters and riders of non-motorised scooters still had to always give way to cyclists. They, however, were permitted to share cycling lanes with bicycle riders but only outside the peak cycle-travelling times of 6:00 a.m. to 9:00 a.m. and 3:00 p.m. to 6:00 p.m. (Monday to Friday).

During the peak cycle travelling times, roller skaters and riders of non-motorised scooters were only permitted to travel on pedestrian footpaths at a speed paralleled with a brisk walking pace, typically about five kilometres per hour.

Throughout Borebland, but particularly in the suburb of Hiptoun, most thoroughfares for motorised vehicles were either one-way streets or laneways. All streets, though, had a cycling lane on either side. Cyclists, therefore, could ride in either direction.

The one-lane thoroughfare for motor vehicles was only wide enough for the lone vehicle. The standard-sized cycling lanes, however, were wide enough for at least three cyclists to ride abreast. Note: cyclists easily outnumbered motor vehicle drivers.

Small to medium-sized trucks and vans were only allowed in and out of Hiptoun by one of the three heavily patrolled checkpoints. Any attempt to enter the suburb via any other means meant a heavy fine and an impoundment of the vehicle.

The vehicle's owner, whether it be an individual or a company, then had to pay another monetary fine to retrieve it from the impoundment yard, located behind the fortified Law Enforcement and Compliance building complex.

For a truck or van to pass through the checkpoint, the driver needed to provide evidence that the vehicle was either *green certified* or *green credentialled.*

No diesel-driven vehicles (semi-trailers for example) were ever allowed into Hiptoun, South Duffel or Bunnslich. Most transport vehicles, such as small to medium-sized trucks and vans, were hybrid vehicles that combined a petrol engine with an electric motor.

The cycling gangs had managed to build up a favourable reputation throughout the Borebland shire over many years and had even earned a 'healthy aura of reverence' amongst the local populace.

Numerous murals in Hiptoun were dedicated to past and current pioneering cycling 'heroes' – especially the ones that once had close ties or connections to local government bodies or well-known community groups.

Despite a history of turf wars (both violent and non-violent) between the eight cycling gangs, they would still often cycle together every Sunday morning, a pastime that became known as *The Sunday Cycle*.

Typically, between 7:00 a.m. and 10:00 a.m., members from each of the gangs would cycle together as a 'gesture of cordial unity' along the main thoroughfares and even along some of the back streets and laneways/alleys – six to eight abreast.

Easily identifiable by the colour of their Lycra outfits, individuals casually chatted amicably amongst themselves whilst motor vehicles could only drive patiently behind them.

Motorists dared not to use their car horns as this would result in a heavy fine being imposed upon them. The use of a car horn was illegal in the Borebland shire. Cyclists, however, were free to use warning bells or bicycle horns at any time!

After the Sunday social morning ride, most cycling gang members would later join the Sunday Protests and participate in various 'Beware of Cyclists' campaigns.

Additionally, they would pay a special homage to the current female Green Gaia (the mayor) by chanting a well-learned mantra quite passionately and exuberantly, thanking her for the continual and prosperous cycling conditions that they deeply cherished!

7 In Pursuit of Trivia

Throughout the suburbs of Covidorne, pub trivia nights were plentiful (and well patronised) and none more so than the spectacular trivia events in Borebland. The ever-shriving pub culture meant that there was a plethora of entertainment choices. Trivia nights took place nightly from Monday to Thursday (and Sunday afternoons) at multiple hotel venues.

Charlie's obsession with trivia began well and truly before the day he relocated to the suburb of Hiptoun. In his childhood (especially during his teenage years), Charlie regularly buried himself in encyclopaedia pages and later onto online trivia. Furthermore, he was an avid long-term fan (to the point of near fanaticism at times) of any television trivia or quiz game shown throughout his younger years. In his hometown of Ratatatatutra, however, pub trivia was yet to be discovered.

Courtesy of several Spirit of Wokeness building complex residents, Charlie was quickly exposed to the enthralment of Borebland's thriving pub culture extravaganza: especially in the suburbs of Hiptoun, South Duffel, Ritzsoy and Bunnslich.

Pub trivia events were popular and well supported by many of Borebland's residents (and non-residents) – even when held at multiple venues simultaneously. Alek believed there were at least fifteen hotel venues to choose from on Thursday nights alone!

Two weeks after settling into Hiptoun, Charlie attended his first pub trivia night at the Manni Sack Hotel in Bunnslich as part of a team that consisted of Floozie, Hazelle, Angelica, and Lazer.

Most trivia events were organised and hosted by a well-established trivia company, whilst in-house trivia events (usually organised and hosted by hotel management or staff) rarely took place.

On Charlie's second trivia night, the entertaining event was organised by the *Smart Alek Trivia Company* – hosted by Alek. Yes, it was his company!

With rotating orb lights and loud-playing 'retro' music, Alek entered the room on a pair of flashing disco-lighted roller skates – and to thunderous applause. The trivia event consisted of two rounds of general knowledge, a picture round, and a music round.

The entertainment extravaganza lasted for just over two hours. The venue was packed (80+ people) and tables of trivia teams were packed in like sardines. Charlie's team did quite well that night, ending up in third place out of eighteen teams.

Charlie quickly learnt that trivia 'grandmaster' Alek had a devoted cult following, hosting trivia events on Tuesday, Wednesday and Thursday nights. He would also host the occasional corporate trivia event on Friday and Saturday nights, mainly fundraising for a designated charity or a worthy cause.

Trivia night hosting for Alek was a secondary source of income, but a financially lucrative one. His primary source of income was part-time employment (three or four days a week) in a 'continental' cheese-making factory in Bunnslich.

Charlie (the following week) attended trivia events over four consecutive nights: Monday to Thursday.

On Monday night, he casually wandered into the Figjam Hotel (Hiptoun) to participate in a trivia night. In stark contrast to the Manni Sack Hotel in Bunnslich, there were fewer teams and, thus, fewer participants (twenty-eight altogether).

After consuming a discounted 'Monday night special' meal, Charlie was ready for pub trivia – on his own.

Two hours later, he had survived the onslaught of forty-five trivia questions which, at times, truly tested the part of his brain that contained a 'multitude' of trivia facts that had previously been resting peacefully!

Charlie soon realised that participating in a trivia night as a solo team was quite daunting and somewhat stressful; his brain was in an active turbo-mode for *every* question.

Three of the teams had five or more players. In the end, Charlie came in fourth position (out of eight teams), just five points behind the victorious seven-person team.

The following night, Charlie attended another pub trivia event at the Jale Prey Hotel in the suburb of Ritzsoy. As a solo player again, he encountered a set of trivia questions (over two rounds) that certainly tested his 'grey matter' to the ultimate level. Out of thirteen teams, Charlie finished tenth.

After the first few questions, however, Charlie presumed that he was competing against teams of veteran *trivia diehards*. All teams consisted of players over thirty years of age, with at least half of the participants aged over fifty.

Charlie presumed that most participants were well-established 'trivia combatants' who had been participating in trivia events for years *or* perhaps even for several decades.

Before the commencement of the trivia event, Charlie enjoyed an old-styled and distinctly home-cooked mixed-grill dinner. The vegetables (potatoes, pumpkin, onion, beans, and peas) were oven-roasted but only covered about a third of the large plate. The other two-thirds (of the plate) consisted of several mouth-watering types of meat: thick slices of beef steak, lamb chops, pork sausages and beef mince patties.

During the trivia event, Charlie occasionally glanced at his fellow trivia combatants. Closest to his small table was a group of six people – all were only drinking water.

There were three water jugs on their table. Although Charlie didn't know what their team name was, he thought: 'The *Aquarians* or the *Water Bearers* would be an appropriate choice!'

In the middle of the hotel, sat a group of twelve people around a long table. Charlie figured that (at least) half of the team was aged over sixty. It soon became apparent that only several (trivia) players seemed to be actively involved in the trivia game!

The rest seem contented to only eat homemade biscuits and cakes, accompanied by several bottles of wine. They would chat idly amongst themselves, appearing to have little interest in contributing to the required amount of teamwork necessary to provide the correct answer (or answers) to each given question.

Close to Charlie's table was a group of four middle-aged females, all attired in clothing that could be described as *retrobohemian.*

Two of these ladies were 'dressed to the nines' as portrayed by their unique and flamboyant dress sense. As with the other two women, they looked like they had also had a recent beauty parlour makeover – plenty of makeup, along with 'creative and fashionable' hair designs.

A couple of weeks later, though, Charlie learnt they were all involved in the fashion design industry and possessed a special penchant for retro-style clothing.

Adjacent to the large team seated around the long table in the middle of the hotel, sat three burly late-middle-aged gentlemen clustered around a small table pushed up against the wall. Their table was the closest to the service bar area.

Although casually dressed, all three belonged to a motorcycle gang, in one of Borebland's neighbouring shires (Darewin).

Their Harley Davidson motorcycles were parked in a specially designated area on the street that was cordoned off by several large, orange-coloured witches' hats, close to the hotel's main entrance.

Charlie would soon learn that this team, as with several other teams, had been participating in this trivia event for over a decade!

Before the start of each Tuesday night trivia event, all three would order the same food and drink every week: the mixed-grilled dinner and a jug of beer (each). They were super-competitive and treated the trivia event quite seriously.

They analysed, debated, and relentlessly discussed *every* single question. Using the name 'WTF' they were, however, the team to beat each week; even if they were starting the trivia event on a minus-five handicap, due to being victorious the previous week.

Charlie participated in this Tuesday night trivia event at the Jale Prey Hotel as a solo player (for three weeks) before joining another team: *Norfolk and Chance.*

Team 'Norfolk and Chance' consisted of six players (but rarely had a full team each week) and alternated between the Jale Prey Hotel and the Miker Piker Hotel in Barfton.

The following night (Wednesday), Charlie participated in a trivia event held at the Canny Spam Hotel in South Duffel. The previous two nights, he had used the name Going Solo as his team's name but on this occasion, Charlie decided on a new team name: C.R.A.F.T at Trivia.

On this night, Charlie was pitted against nine other teams. Halfway through the trivia night, he was in third place and only two points behind the leading team.

When the answers were read out after the second round, Charlie realised that he had scored thirty-eight points out of (a possible) forty points and thought to himself: 'I have a good chance of winning this.' He was right and won by three points!

Before leaving the venue, however, Charlie was casually approached and then 'recruited' by a rival team. The friendly group (seated at a neighbouring table) had chatted with him throughout the evening. The team also preferred to alternate between different venues (just like Charlie's Tuesday team of trivia boffins), but on a three-week rotational cycle instead.

Charlie continued to play trivia on Monday nights at the Figjam Hotel as a solo player for a further three weeks. In the fifth week, however, he had managed to persuade Alek and Lazer to join him. Several players from his newly-found Tuesday and Wednesday trivia groups also joined.

After five weeks of playing hotel trivia, Charlie wasn't participating in any of the pub events as a solo player. He was now part of a different team on all four nights.

Charlie, though, would (occasionally) participate in a trivia event as a solo player, once again using the team name C.R.A.F.T at Trivia.

This would only occur if his fellow team members had decided, for example, to attend a special event such as the *Covidorne International Comedy Extravaganza* (in Hiptoun) or were away during holiday periods or due to community health hazards (e.g. influenza).

Charlie never succumbed to any illness, however, as his passion for trivia events *always* came first and would, thus, override any potential health issues!

Over the next several months, all four trivia groups would develop a reputation as being quite formidable opponents to all other competing teams. On Monday nights, Charlie's team only attended the trivia event at the Figjam Hotel. On the other three trivia nights, the teams alternated between multiple venues, located throughout the shire of Borebland.

All trivia events handed out prizes, usually in the form of vouchers. Prizes were for the first three placegetters or just the first two placegetters. But other vouchers were awarded throughout the night, usually for a jug of beer or a bottle of wine. Several trivia venues also had a jackpot round.

To win the jackpot, a team had to answer correctly three harder-than-normal questions and if none of the teams could answer all three questions correctly that night, the jackpot prize pool would accumulate to the next trivia event.

It could take weeks before the jackpot prize was finally won. The successful team would then be awarded vouchers from fifty to several hundred dollars.

All four of Charlie's teams would regularly win vouchers. This, in turn, meant lots of free meals and alcoholic beverages, equating to a cheap night out or even the occasional free one.

Charlie's level of trivia knowledge (well above average) was certainly appreciated by his teammates, and it did not take long for opposing teams (on all four trivia nights) to realise that he was one of the 'central cogs' within each of his teams!

Some of his trivia teammates (and even some of the players in rival teams) had previously participated in several different television quiz game shows.

At the time, two quiz shows (on rival television channels) were on the air. A few of the trivia players had participated in at least one of these televised game shows; three of them had even been fortunate enough to receive a boost to their bank account after their successful television appearance!

Charlie was urged by both his teammates (and rival trivia players) to apply to these quiz-game television shows. He was, however, more interested in entering another contest within the next couple of years or so: the annually-held International Quiz Championship in early June.

8 Niches of Entertainment

The vibrant uniqueness of the entertainment scene within Borebland presented a vast array of choices. From stand-up comedy, theatre productions, indie/alternative music gigs, and 'talent' shows, there was *something for everyone.*

Musical acts, theatre productions and other forms of entertainment often attracted certain people who commonly became known as 'nichies'. These so-called niche audiences were prominent at various venues throughout the suburbs of Borebland.

Hiptoun was the hub of the Borebland entertainment scene, particularly the niche (entertainment). Although the Covidorne International Comedy Festival shows were held in numerous venues, most were in Hiptoun.

Other shows were held in the nearby suburbs of Bunnslich, Ritzsoy, and South Duffel. Several of the stand-up comedians were either based or lived within one of these four suburbs as well.

One of these stand-up comedians was Alek, the debonair trivia host. For several years, he had tried to prove himself within the oft-challenging stand-up comedy scene. Alas, success for him would be somewhat limited but his relentless passion rarely ever waned. Alek would still perform at any opportune moment, particularly at the events that attracted overseas-based stand-up comedians.

For the past three years, Alek had been one of the locally-chosen performers at the internationally-acclaimed annual Borebland Comedy Festival: one of Covidorne's major events for the year.

Whilst not as financially lucrative as trivia hosting or his part-time employment in a local cheese-making factory, Alek believed that the stand-up comedy scene was, at the very least, a fulfilling side project.

Many theatre houses in Borebland were in operation each week. Although the low-budget stage plays attracted regular audiences, they were no match for the thriving and long-established improvised comedy scene.

Hotels in the suburbs of Hiptoun, Bunnslich, and South Duffel provided the necessary floor space (and a stage) for troupes of impro-comedy performers.

The main venue for improvised comedy was in Piranha, a suburb in Mockington Shire (a bordering shire of Borebland).

Theatre performances took place there every Sunday evening and attracted much larger audiences (up to three hundred attendees) compared to the hotel venues which were generally limited to about 50-80 people.

Angelica, Floozie, and Hazelle had been long-time and avid supporters of the thriving impro-comedy scene, long before Charlie's big move from the small town of Ratatatatutra to the vibrant capital city of Covidorne. After just two weeks, he joined them one Sunday evening.

The weekly impro-comedy productions in Piranha took place during four specially-themed seasonal blocks: *Sizzlin' Summer, Anarchy Autumn, Wacky Winter,* and *Sensuous Spring.*

Lasting for about two months, each seasonal block was also intermittently divided by a rest period of four weeks. Charlie would be a notable regular at these theatrical performances; a commitment that would last for him over the next two and a half years.

Charlie conversed with the acting performers from time to time but would never get to know any of them on a personal level. A few months later, he would recognise several of them in television commercials that advertised insurance options (car, life, etc.), toothpaste brands, soap brands and even short-term financial loan advertisements.

Several members of the impro-comedy family had even progressed to the 'silver screen' albeit in minor roles and only in Austrutopian productions.

Despite its consistent popularity, the improvised comedy scene still found itself regularly competing against other forms of entertainment, some of which could be best described as bizarre or 'unique'.

The Marcel Marceau Appreciation Society (MMAS) steadily enjoyed increasing membership and popularity over many years. The performing mime artists would participate in different formats of entertainment events such as street festivals, variety nights and street-performing buskers.

Several years ago, the MMAS had been granted the use of Hiptoun Community Hall. Besides organising and conducting regular miming workshops for current society members to develop or hone their skills, the premises also functioned as a place to attract potential or would-be mime artists.

The workshops, inadvertently, soon evolved beyond their main purpose and became more of a thriving social outlet. Close friendships were formed, an important aspect where several or many members could be banded together and, thus, form a cohesive professional group of performers.

These groups would regularly launch themselves at the unsuspecting public whether it would be on the streets, in shopping centres, in parks or even in eateries and hotels.

Although the main purpose of the mime artists was to be entertaining and just have fun, they also used this opportunity to promote the Marcel Marceau Appreciation Society and any of their upcoming gigs such as street festivals, revues, comedy festivals, etc. And then there were the frequent 'talent' shows!

The Talent Shows could be described as 'no-holds-barred' variety events. Mostly hosted by a stand-up comedian, these performance events were held in a small to medium-sized room with a small stage (or raised platform) and often within a dining restaurant or hotel dining area.

A diverse range of talented performers would then *strut their stuff*. A few of these performers managed to make a decent income from their 'talents' but for the majority, the performances were just a part-time project (or an enjoyable pastime).

Sleight-of-hand magicians seemed to be in plentiful supply. A situation that Charlie was led to believe that it may have even been compulsory to have at least one magician at each entertainment show or gig!

Then there were the different types of jugglers: the standard ones juggling three or four objects; those that juggled objects whilst balancing on a unicycle; a mixture of acrobatics and juggling; and bizarrely, the occasional individual that combined the 'art' of stripping with juggling. But there were still other types of niche performers as well!

Storytellers, poets (particularly slam poetry performers), puppeteers, and ventriloquists would occasionally 'grace the stage'.

The storytellers would often share with their compelling audiences a wide range of first-hand recollections, ranging from for example: recent (or not so recent) international or domestic travel adventures; Centrelink experiences (e.g. having access to or approval of social security payments); and even to the 'life and times' of a beloved pet such as a python, a guinea pig, a dog, a cat, a goldfish, etc.

The quirky poets were quite a fascinating lot. Often attired like artists of a bygone era (e.g., the metro-Bohemian look), they had gradually achieved a cult-like following over many years, particularly on university or technical college campus grounds. Many professional poets began their careers at these types of venues.

Enthusiastic audiences ensured that recitals of popular-known poems (often penned decades or centuries ago) would be well-received.

It was the enthralling presentation of original material, however, that would decide whether the aspiring poet would be futuristically successful or not. Successful ones were even able to eke out a decent income, especially on the slam poetry professional circuit which was mostly held on spacious campus grounds or major indoor venues.

Slam poetry commonly combines elements of poetry, theatre, performance, and storytelling. At the end of the recital performance, the poet received a score.

In line with Borebland's *everyone is a winner* policy, every participant received a trophy. Only a select few, however, would receive a cash prize.

Peer-pressured by several of the residents in the Spirit of Wokeness complex (Angelica, Floozie and Hazelle), Charlie was soon a regular attendee at many of these talent or variety shows.

Besides magicians, jugglers, storytellers, and poets there were other entertaining performers. These included acrobats and non-categorised performing artists.

The dying art of puppetry was rarely part of any show or event, and the odd aspiring puppeteer tended to only use hand-held puppets in what may be best described as an old-style vaudeville setup, uncannily like a traditional Punch and Judy show!

There was the occasional puppet-on-a-string show where the puppeteer (or puppeteers) hovered above the performing puppets and were visible to the audience. The audience, at times, seemed to be more entertained by the facial expressions of the puppeteers than the actual puppet show!

Ventriloquists, on the other hand, were exceptionally talented. Charlie believed these 'niche-skilled' individuals may have practised tirelessly in the bedroom (or in the basement) of their family home for years and in their younger days.

From performing initially to just family and close friends, these aspiring and highly motivated ventriloquists eventually progressed to showing their unique talent to audiences on a much wider scale.

Although ventriloquists rarely appeared at talent/variety shows, they were nevertheless often billed as the main act (as displayed on posters or billboards) and, thus, considered a major drawcard to attract a sizeable audience.

Over several years, Charlie only ever saw a handful of these talented performers as they were largely part of an extensive worldwide travelling entertainment circuit and performed in international competitions, on the 'big screen' (e.g., television programs) and at larger venues – even on cruise ships as well.

The most popular form of entertainment throughout the Borebland shire, however, was the seemingly non-stop live music scene.

Indie bands (indie-rock, indie-pop, indie-folk, etc.) played in a multitude of venues every single night and during the day on weekends, particularly throughout the suburbs of Hiptoun, Bunnslich, Barfton, Ritzsoy, Nobberk and South Duffel.

Although indie music dominated the musical landscape, there were other music genres as well, even uncategorised ones best described as being 'experimental'.

Disc jockeys and sound improvisers were never overly popular throughout Borebland Shire and, thus, appeared to be mostly 'shadow-banned' in Hiptoun!

Somehow, they managed to attract devoted 'nichies' to their shows, particularly in the lesser-known suburbs of Borebland Shire. Financially, it was still worthwhile for them to continue to perform.

Many hotel venues (and several restaurants as well) often supplied two types of entertainment throughout the night, particularly on Thursday, Friday, and Saturday nights.

For example, some hotels would stage a trivia event say between 7:00 p.m. and 9:00 p.m. and then follow on with live music or the two events would slightly overlap each other.

The two different forms of entertainment, however, tended to only attract separate groups of attendees. As soon as the trivia event ended, most of the 'trivia combatants' headed for the exits, walking straight past the live entertainment. A few people, however, attended the trivia event and then stayed afterwards for the live entertainment.

At Bunnlich's Manni Sack Hotel on Thursday nights, the team of Charlie, Floozie, Hazelle, Angelica and Lazer would participate in the trivia event (in the undercover beer garden) between 8:00 p.m. and 9:45 p.m. Live music generally started in the main bar around 9:30 p.m.

Once the trivia event had ended, most of the (trivia) participants passed through the main bar and exited the hotel. Charlie suspected that the hotel was trying to lure the trivia participants into staying in the main bar and, thus, purchasing more drinks.

The indie bands and other musical performers appeared to be mostly novices, possibly performing outside of a house garage or basement for the first time!

One night, as Charlie and his four trivia teammates walked through the main bar, a performing act was trying to combine poetry and rapping, along with making bizarre noises on creatively-made instruments that appeared to be made from numerous household items such as pots, saucepans, empty coffee (or milo) tins, rolling pins, spoons, wine glasses and even aluminium baking trays.

Many trivia players just shook their heads as they walked past, whilst a small group of retro-bohemian enthusiasts were standing close to the front of the stage and in a zombie-like trance, gently swayed or moved 'carefreely' to a somewhat imaginary beat!

Charlie thought: 'I don't think I'd even last five minutes listening to this stuff' and then instantly exclaimed, 'What the hell is this?'

Hazelle coolly responded, 'Something only a *niche audience* could understand and appreciate!'

The better-known indie bands (and other popular musical acts) played regularly on Friday and Saturday nights. Many bands performed original musical compositions, although others were primarily cover bands.

Eventually, some musical acts managed to go onto better and brighter futures. Venturing on national tours (and even international ones) and along with sales of albums and streaming services, these bands would morph into becoming full-time professional musicians.

Many had emerged from humble beginnings, even from the Thursday night gigs at the Manni Sack Hotel!

9 The Community-Spirited Groups

Borebland Shire had long been regarded as a prosperous sanctuary for numerous community-spirited groups. The major groups (in particular) were well-known throughout the capital city of Covidorne.

Even Borebland's official motto reflected this concept: *The Shire of Woke Progressiveness and Community Spirit.*

Consecutive Green Gaia supremos actively encouraged everyone, throughout the shire of Borebland, to be part of the overall vibe of 'community togetherness and tolerance'.

Besides the numerous posters and several large billboards placed quite sporadically throughout the suburbs, local radio stations regularly encouraged residents to join a group – or even several groups.

Initially, the community-spirited groups were formed on the concept of 'social awareness' and focused on several core values: acceptance, friendliness, togetherness, participation, and *positive* activism. Despite the good intentions, it didn't take long for these concepts of well-meaning ideas to develop into what may be best described as *attention-seeking wokeism.*

Whilst there were many community-spirited groups throughout Borebland, the shire was noticeably dominated by the five largest ones: Witchy Bitches Femo Club; Warring Vegans Social Club; Tofu and T-Bone Reconciliation Society;

the Beef and Beer Bogan Pride Association; and Anarchy International.

The vast majority of residents throughout the Borebland Shire (especially in the suburbs of Hiptoun, Bunnslich, South Duffel, Barfton, Nobberk and Ritzsoy) were members of one or more of these major 'community-spirited' groups.

The Witchy Bitches Femo Club (WBFC) socialised mostly through regular *grievance meetings* or proactive participation in the numerous street protests. As Lazer had previously told Charlie: 'The grievance meetings are simply just winge and whine sessions!'

Some of the WBFC meetings were held in one of the conference rooms of the Spirit of Wokeness building complex, typically once a week. Advertised as a social event or as an 'amicable' get-together, the female organisers and attendees soon ensured that the meeting would generally end up being quite boisterous and an 'over-the-top winge fest'!

At the front of the room, there was a lectern. The first speaker was the president of the WBFC. Her primary role was to welcome the attendees and then announce the upcoming agenda of the meeting.

Next up was the vice president who would then deliver an introductory speech that outlined the topics to be discussed.

Members of the audience would then be invited to the lectern to air their views (or grievances) within a time limit of five minutes.

Whilst a few aspiring orators brought notes with them, most were comfortable just ad-libbing during their time at the lectern.

The topics discussed at each meeting consistently focus on certain concepts such as female superiority, the curse of white male privilege and (supposed) male chauvinism.

After each speaker finished their *tirade of passion*, scenes of overzealous exuberance, amid frantic handclapping and even hysterical screams of approval added to the effervescent aura that flowed positively throughout the conference room. The clamorous noise could even be heard throughout the complex and the immediate neighbourhood!

Lazer and others at one time, tried to stand in the corridor and eavesdrop on these 'sociable' events – until security was deployed.

Two oversized and heavily tattooed women with short, blue-rinsed hair and along with numerous body piercings (lips, ears, nose, eyelids, and easily visible bellybuttons), patrolled the corridors with 'iron' fists and laced-up jackboots!

Nevertheless, the male occupants of the Spirit of Wokeness building complex were regularly informed of the proceedings of these meetings courtesy of Angelica, Floozie and Hazelle (regular attendees). Moo never attended though.

Whilst Angelica and Floozie enthusiastically supported the general agenda of the WBFC, Hazelle was inclined to view the meetings more as 'spectacles of entertainment'. She regularly informed Lazer and Charlie (with a certain degree of sarcasm) about the issues being debated and discussed.

Whilst the WBFC was proactive in indoor settings, they were equally proactive outdoors as well – especially within the activist utopian world of street protests.

As a substantial percentage of the WBFC were regular participants in the weekly Sunday protests, they soon earned a 'badge of respect' from the Sunday Protest movement.

They were the first group to lead the extravagant parade along Kiddenee Road, chanting hysterically well-rehearsed mantras centring on several themes: the power of women's positivity; why women are underprivileged; and, why they do not like 'toxic' masculinity.

The WBFC would occasionally organise *women-only* street protests and hysterically chant the types of themes that were similarly voiced at the Sunday protests. Other like-minded groups also participated in these protests from time to time, even if it was just for supportive purposes.

Participants in these street rallies would eventually gather together on the parliament steps in central Covidorne.

Emotionless Green Gaia security officers, distinguished by their grass-green uniforms (and several red arm bands), along with red caps and laced-up red boots, casually stood in front of the entrances of the parliament building and guarded against any would-be intruders.

With 'talented' musicians using bongos, tambourines and whistles, several individuals with megaphones ranted with passionate exuberance to their over-enthusiastic audience.

Lasting for over an hour, the over-zealous fanfare would end abruptly, and the masses departed peacefully, chatting excitedly amongst themselves.

The Warring Vegans Social Club (WVSC) consisted mostly of females (including non-gender types identifying as women) but at least twenty per cent of members were males.

A large percentage of the female members also belonged to the WBFC, whilst a small percentage of male members were also involved in the Tofu and T-bone Reconciliation Society.

Staunchly opposed to any consumption of meat, especially red meats such as beef and lamb, the WVSC would only promote plant-based foods such as vegan sausages, vegan burgers, so-called 'smart' food (tofu, kimchi, bean sprouts, etc) and other uncharacterised 'ethical' foodstuffs.

At one time, the WVSC was quite a bitter rival to the *Anarchy International* (AI) and the *Beef and Beer Bogan Pride Association* (BABBPA) groups. They even engaged in physical altercations with these two groups from time to time.

The lean and fit (but light-weighted) WVSC members, however, were no match for the well-fed and heavily built members of BABBPA. Nor did they fare that well against members of AI who were experienced 'street combatants.'

A truce was now a necessity; one that would be achieved through the creation of the Tofu and T-bone Reconciliation Society (TTBRS).

The local Fabrication News Channel One (FNC1), owned by the Borebland Shire Council, were initially dismayed with these conciliatory measures as they felt the skirmishes (even the violent ones) made 'good' television!

Additionally, the acts of street violence fitted in perfectly with their agenda (or official narrative) that the Beef and Beer Bogan Pride Association members were primarily a group of 'uncouth far right-wing thugs'.

The FNC1, nevertheless, mostly viewed the physical skirmishes between the Warring Vegans Social Club and the Anarchy International community groups as nothing more than just a 'misunderstanding' over fundamental differences between the two groups.

As these street skirmishes between the warring groups managed to score above-average viewing ratings within the Borebland Shire and neighbouring shires, taxpayer-funded *ideas consultants* employed by FNC1 soon produced what they thought was a 'brilliant' idea.

After meeting with the hierarchy of the three groups (WVSC, AI and BABBPA), the FNC1's ideas consultants then outlined their planned strategy for the three groups to conduct mock physical altercations during street protests.

Before the next scheduled street protest was to take place, the warring community groups undertook several rehearsal sessions, in an endeavour to develop and hone the 'art' of fake combatting.

During the next so-called 'peaceful' street protest, there were plenty of scripted physical skirmishes. The enthusiastic combatants engaged mainly in the following: swinging their arms wildly near the heads of opponents; regularly falling to the ground but quickly 'recovered' in readiness for the next round of combatant activities; and plenty of 'claret' (fake blood) was sneakily thrown at physical torsos and clothing.

The FNC1 news reporters and video cameras were quickly on the scene and the 'violent events' of the street protest were the main item on FNC1's 6:00 p.m. prime news timeslot. As a result, the audience ratings were favourably high for the FNC1 television network that evening!

The Tofu and T-bone Reconciliation Society (TATRS) were quite an intriguing community group. The creation of the group emerged from the popular desire to harmonise the *cultural differences* between the devout vegan community and the 'carnivore community' (a term coined for members of BABBPA).

Whilst the vegans steadfastly opposed the consumption of meat, they reluctantly decided to respect the culinary choices of dedicated meat lovers – even those who devoured red meat daily or almost daily.

Lazer was a passionate member of TATRS. He enjoyed devouring all types of food: vegan, vegetarian, or meat-based. An equally enthusiastic Charlie joined the group as well. His culinary tastes were similar to Lazer's.

A regular red meat eater, courtesy of his childhood upbringing, Charlie was introduced to tofu and other *vegan delights* by Floozie – a prominent 'vegan aficionado'. Tofu was certainly one of her favourite foods and to sway people like Charlie away from meat-based choices, she occasionally offered him flavoured baked or fried pieces of tofu (curry was a favourite of hers).

Charlie also enjoyed cooking and had developed a unique method of 'culinary experimentation' where he would fry or bake chunks (either thin or large) of tofu in the delicious juices of several types of red meat such as T-bone steaks, whole roast lamb, beef, or turkey and even sausages.

One evening, Charlie knocked on Floozie's front door and offered her a sample of his *culinary vision* only to be met with an emphatic NO and an immediate slam of the door!

Anarchy International (AI) was one of the early-established community-spirited groups within the shire of Borebland. It was also part of a wider worldwide network.

AI's headquarters was a restored abandoned warehouse in Hiptoun but in several nearby suburbs, they also had meeting places, typically in private homes or community halls. These meeting places were colloquially known as 'cells'.

The group was well known throughout Covidorne and quickly developed a reputation for protesting – and violence.

To an outsider, most of its members seem to have an endless passion for rowdy protesting and street fighting.

Initially, they just engaged in physical and sometimes violent combat with rival groups, especially with the Beef and Beer Bogan Pride Association (BABBPA).

One problem though. A small percentage of individuals belonged to *both* groups. Lazer for example. He and others would just simply switch sides on an alternating basis for each upcoming street battle!

As aforementioned, the local Fabrication News Channel One (FNC1) managed to persuade the combatting groups to only engage in (well-scripted) physical skirmishes on certain adrenalin-fuelled protest days.

A grassy area behind AI's headquarters warehouse (and well hidden from public view) was used for training sessions involving the concept of 'fake fighting.' Elements of military-styled combat were employed but previously televised worldwide wrestling entertainment shows appeared to have been more of an influence on these combative sessions!

Aside from their active participation in numerous street protests, Anarchy International was clearly defined by a stoic philosophical charter that included several key core beliefs centring on being anti-religious and pro-atheist; generally being anti-government as they disliked any political party; and being *anti-establishment* as they opposed the wealthy elite.

Within the warehouse, there was a large room that sold a wide range of merchandise, connected in at least some way to the worldwide anarchism movement whether it was literature material, posters, music, toys – or even makeshift weapons for confrontational street protests.

Members of Anarchy International were notorious for their regular noisy sit-down protests on the front steps of the Borebland Council building complex. Strangely enough, they were peacefully tolerated by council members and local law enforcement officers, where the latter was colloquially known as the 'Green Gaia Hit Squad' (GGHS).

The GGHS were easily identifiable by their prominent red and black uniform (and green armbands on the upper part of the sleeves). Sympathisers amongst council members and the GGHS would often bow their heads in front of the protesters and present them with white or yellow flowers as a gesture of 'goodwill' friendship and tolerance!

These 'peaceful' protestors of Anarchy International and other communal groups would occasionally glue themselves to the street tarmac in front of or near the council buildings, emphasising the 'urgency' of a particular grievance issue.

Traffic (mostly bicycles) would be diverted around them, but the protestors were only allowed to lie (glued) on the road for up to an hour.

After an hour, any remaining non-complying diehards were met with bucket loads of specially formulated soaps and water from high-pressure hoses; a course of action designed to 'unglue' them from the bitumen surface.

Small fines were occasionally handed out, but the GGHS mostly resorted to the symbolic gesture of slapping them gently on the wrist with their hand and passionately urging them not to do it again!

Although the Anarchy International community group boasted of being the largest group membership-wise (many also belonging to one of the bicycle gangs) and one of the most influential ones within the Borebland shire, they were constantly being challenged by the ever-increasingly brazen Beef and Beer Bogan Pride Association – their bitter rivals.

BABBPA initially began with a small membership but soon attracted a constant stream of new members; especially younger people relocating from the rural regions of Luzerstan to the capital city of Covidorne for either employment or further educational purposes.

Charlie was introduced to several key BABBPA members by Lazer, less than three weeks after moving to Hiptoun from Ratatatatutra and soon joined the group.

Lazer was the then-treasurer of BABBPA and first introduced Charlie to Warren, who was commonly known as 'Wazza'. Wazza was the president and had a substantial criminal record that began in his 'juvenile delinquent' years.

BABBPA's *dress code* consisted of several easily identifiable characteristics: checked-coloured flannelette shirts; numerous body and occasional facial tattoos; mullet or mohawk-styled haircuts; and black-leather boots (jackboots were popular).

Although there was a steady flow of new members, BABBPA was still smaller than fellow combatant community groups such as Anarchy International (AI) and the Warring Vegans Social Club (WVSC).

When it came to street battles, though, the often-outnumbered BABBPA members had little difficulty in either 'holding their own' or even defeating one of their main adversaries. As they were *passionate* meat-eaters and avid beer drinkers, most of the members were physically larger and stronger than their opposing counterparts.

Most of the BABBPA members also spent a healthy amount of time in gyms, lifting weights or sparring in one of the boxing rings. The latter activity was often a precursor to any upcoming planned or occasionally unplanned street battle.

The group regarded the street battles as entertainment for the cameras, whether for FNC1 or even for the onlookers recording the combatant spectacle with their mobile phones.

Although the increasing membership was mostly due to individuals relocating from rural cities and towns within the state of Luzerstan, the original core of the group consisted of city-raised individuals who eventually merged, coming from smaller groups such as the Patriot Brothers and Sisters, United Patriot Movement and Patriots Rule.

A previous Borebland Green Gaia Supremo, however, had decided to introduce legislation outlawing the use of the word 'patriot' in the name of any community group. As a result, the three groups merged, thus, creating a more 'name-friendly' group: Beef and Beer Bogan Pride Association (BABBPA).

Although female membership of BABBPA was originally quite minuscule (less than ten per cent), the ratio between the two sexes over the years steadily narrowed. When Charlie decided to join this group, the ratio was about 65% male and 35% female.

The then vice president was Sharon (better known as 'Shazza') and like most of the other females in the group, she often mirrored the appearance and behaviour of her male counterparts.

For example, Sharon's favourite meal was steak (especially T-bone), fried potato chips and beer. A professional boxer and a mixed martial arts (MMA) fighter, she also sported a typical 1980s mullet-like hairstyle and often wore a flannelette shirt, along with a pair of blue jeans and black leather steel-capped boots.

Like her male counterparts, Shazza (as with other female members) also enjoyed participating in the street skirmishes, even battling against the males at times – especially those belonging to the Warring Vegans Social Club.

10 Vegan Viral Mania

As the wintry conditions gradually took hold of the Borebland shire and with the onset of the traditional influenza season, a strange phenomenon began to unfold. A certain section of the Borebland community appeared to be suffering far worse from the seasonal strains of the flu than other communal members – the vegan community.

Tales of the ailing vegan community experiencing worse-than-normal adverse reactions to the season's influenza strain soon dominated the headlines of various local media outlets.

The local media quickly sensationalised the situation as a *mystery illness,* even declaring that the vegan community was now in a 'hapless' predicament.

The Borebland Pravda immediately coined the mystery illness as the *Vegan Virus.* In the next newspaper publication: 'The Vegan Virus hits the Borebland vegan community like a savage bolt of lightning' is the major headline of the first page!

Despite the mystery illness quickly sweeping throughout the vegan community, the rest of Borebland was seemingly unaffected, albeit with the occasional cough, sneeze, or head cold. Just typical symptoms of a normal influenza season.

Nevertheless, a campaign of 'sympathy and empathy' for devotees of the vegan lifestyle soon began!

The Warring Vegans Social Club (WVSC) received financial support from the shire council almost immediately.

Although other community-spirited groups sympathised and supported this idea, a notable exception was the Beef and Beer Bogan Pride Association (BABBPA).

BABBPA (with support from several smaller independent media groups) casually suggested that the vegan community had succumbed to the onset of the seasonal flu season because of a 'compromised' immune system. They further added that the vegan community's eating habits were largely to blame!

The WVSC quickly drafted a semi-comprehensive plan that would involve what may be best described as a 'theatrical and emphatic' response to BABBPA's outrageous claims.

Assisted by the Born-Again Vegan Ministry, the WVSC organised meetings and workshops, twice a week, inside the Hiptoun Community Hall. The vegan-friendly Piranha-based impro comedy performers provided the workshop tutorials.

To attract an increased level of empathy from the wider community, the participants were soon taught certain 'skills': fake physical collapses in outdoor settings, on the streets and in shopping centres; over-the-top sympathetic responses to collapsed vegan virus 'victims'; and, providing supposedly first aid and medical care (e.g. medications or even mouth-to-mouth resuscitation).

Each workshop concluded with the supportive gesture of everyone holding hands in a human circle, singing the song: *Kumbaya* – albeit with several small changes to the lyrics. For example: 'Hear Me Crying My Lord, Kumbaya' was changed to 'Vegans Are Crying, Kumbaya' and 'Hear Me Praying My Lord, Kumbaya' was now changed to 'Vegans Are Praying, Kumbaya'.

This modified version would also be sung inside the Vegan Reform Church at the start of every service and the end of each service as well!

As aforementioned, non-vegans within the Borebland shire were relatively unscathed by the mystery 'vegan virus' and, a sizable portion of the local population soon adopted quite a sceptical stance towards the supposed authentication of the vegan community's bizarre predicament.

As expected, BABBPA community members were quite cynical and, thus, were not overly impressed with the vegan's attention-seeking theatrical antics in any public area.

Dismayed with the excessive sympathy expressed towards the vegan community, BABBPA decided to commence a campaign of their own: one that centred purely on the health benefits of eating meat – especially beef and lamb.

BABBPAs red meat-eater devotees regularly taunted the hapless vegans by eating chunks of beef or lamb straight off a large bone – in front of them.

The lack of empathy from BABBPA quickly earned the ire of the WVSC (and other supporting groups), culminating in oft-heated verbal exchanges and the occasional physical skirmish between the two community groups. A recent increase of Green Gaia officers on street patrol, however, soon dispelled any nasty fracases between the bitter rivals.

As the weeks rolled on and the weather became colder, the situation of the vegan community seemingly worsened. As a gesture of empathy towards the ailing vegan community, the Borebland council encouraged the Shire's residents to work from home as much as possible.

Many of Borebland's residents also opted to use paid leave (personal leave, annual leave, or long service leave) and, thus, minimise their time spent outside their place of residency.

The newly adopted trend of spending more time inside a residential home soon triggered a variety of changes for Borebland residents when they decided to venture outdoors.

Indoor venues such as shopping centres, cafes and hotels were soon forced to abide by new health and safety regulations implemented by the Borebland Shire Council.

The public transport system, especially the tram network system, quickly saw a steep decline in usage.

Largely influenced by gimmicky advertising, courtesy of local media platforms, many streetwalkers and cyclists began to cover their faces with disposable light blue facemasks.

A substantial quantity of label-free boxes of facemasks (manufactured in an unknown location) had been recently purchased by the Borebland Shire Council.

Some Borebland residents (WVSC members in particular) decided to resort to more extreme measures to protect themselves – wearing a full-face plastic shield or/and even a breathing apparatus over the face mask.

A few individuals, strangely enough, decided to protect themselves even further from the 'despicable disease' by covering most of their bodies with plastic sheeting!

BABBPA and even the Anarchy International (AI) group, meanwhile, scoffed quite aggressively at these over-the-top antics employed by the vegan community.

BABBPA and AI members, in a unified display of blatant defiance, decided to freely roam the streets or use the public transport system without any means of self-protection at all.

As the wintery conditions persisted, crisis meetings were hastily organised to discuss the best course of action to combat and attempt to relieve or halt the physical and mental effects of the 'vegan virus'.

Floozie organised several of these crisis meetings in one of the conference rooms of the Spirit of Wokeness building complex. Before entering the room, though, each attendee had to undergo a body temperature check and provide suitable medical evidence that they were *able-bodied* or in other words, had not succumbed to being a 'vegan virus victim'!

Fellow Spirit of Wokeness residents Moo, Hazelle and Angelica, in support of the ailing vegan community, also attended the Floozie-organised crisis meetings.

At the first meeting, the corridor next to the conference room was an area of eerie silence. Then Lazer and other

BABBPA supporters emerged! Wearing placards front and back of their clothing, they attempted to promote the health benefits of eating red meat.

To add 'theatre' to the now-unwelcomed spectacle, Lazer casually paraded passed the windows and lone entrance of the conference room twice – with a large bone of red meat in one hand and a 750 ml bottle of beer in his other hand.

When he strolled past a third time, Lazer encountered familiar foes – two oversized females with short, blue-rinsed hair wearing grass-green 'Butch Security' uniforms.

They grabbed his arms and dragged him to the outside of his unit. The pair then punched Lazer numerous times in the ribs, the stomach and even several blows to the groin area!

At the next Sunday protest event, the solemn-looking WVSG led the marchers slowly along Kiddenee Road in an attempt to orchestrate an atmosphere of extreme sombreness.

Cladded in various forms of personal safety equipment, such as full-face shields and white-coloured full-body plastic clothing, the ailing 'virus victims' *wailed helplessly* to secure even more empathy from the supportive crowds lining the edges of the street.

Several members of the WVSG carried large cardboard placards: Please Save Us, Support the Ailing Vegans, We Will Overcome and Sympathy for the Hapless Vegan.

At one stage, the marchers came to a halt, and they were met in the middle of the street by the Green Gaia (Borebland council mayor) and her 'entourage' (other councillors) – all dressed in green and red robes of splendour.

Uttering what appeared to be an unintelligible gibberish of nonsense words, the Green Gaia commenced delivering a 'special blessing' to the ailing vegan community. Waving a large rainbow-coloured wand and frequently dipping it into a bowl of an unknown liquid, she then splashed droplets of this 'magical' substance onto the foreheads of the sombre and hapless vegans.

Other major community groups such as the Witchy Bitches Femo Club, Anarchy International and the Tofu and T-Bone Reconciliation Society (but minus most of the T-Bone diehards) also participated in this bizarre march of empathy.

A large contingent of cyclists, attired in their bicycle gang colours, also participated in the march. BABBPA members, meanwhile, casually strolled along behind the marching procession, displaying little empathy towards the 'hapless' vegan community.

Holding placards above their heads with four different messages (Meat Will Save You, Meat Will Make You Better, Long Live Red Meat and Meat Is Best), BABBPA members wore blue jeans and flannelette shirts – most with a beer in one hand and a kebab skewer of lamb in the other.

Charlie, though, decided to be a passive observer and was content to just casually mingle with the large crowd of onlookers. He had declined to participate in this Sunday

Protest, believing that the tense atmosphere could easily morph into one of a volatile and explosive nature. Charlie's gut feeling later proved to be correct!

As with previous Sunday Protests, the marchers strolled through the intersection of Kiddenee Road and Wokespark Avenue, heading towards the Ironic Icon Park Reserve.

Twenty minutes later, security personnel (several burly Pinkerton Mob cyclists) allowed the public to enter through the lone-arched entrance that was surrounded by a perimeter-fenced area.

A few minutes later, the non-marching members of the Tofu and T-Bone Reconciliation Society (TATRS) joined the marching members of the group, and a war of words soon erupted!

The 'tofu wing' of the TATRS angrily expressed their feelings towards the 'T-bone wing' of the group with a barrage of verbal abuse, appalled with the latter's lack of publicly displayed empathy towards the vegan community.

The T-boners then responded, in a mostly calm manner though, that they had the right to choose whether to march or not, adding that most of them had been mingling with supportive onlookers. The fuse, however, was now lit and by the end of the day, the TATRS community group was now bitterly divided and subsequently collapsed.

Over the next three days, two new groups were formed: the Passive T-bone Society (PTS) and the Tofu Patriotic

Association (TPA). Lazer decided to join the newly formed PTS community group, but Charlie chose not to join either group. He had forged healthy friendships with people in both groups and wished to maintain a sense of 'personal neutrality' with them.

The *vegan virus* would linger on for several more weeks. The Borebland Shire Council had approved the production of a locally produced vaccine. Freely available to the vegan community, the 'veganites' slowly recovered.

At one stage, however, the Borebland Pravda ran a sensationalised headline suggesting a batch of vaccines was nothing more than just a placebo and further claimed that the vaccine's contents did little to cure the ailing recipients!

The local newspaper even attempted to drum up further controversy by emphatically suggesting that another batch might have contained animal products (e.g. red meat).

The Green Gaia, however, dismissed these 'outrageous fantasies' and immediately issued a statement, reassuring the vegan community that the vaccines had been *tested extensively* and had been properly secured in a safe place.

As the Borebland Shire began to return to a sense of normality, a far more sinister virus was on its way; one that would be declared as part of a worldwide pandemic. It quickly found its way to the country of Austrutopia via airports and two major seaports.

Predictably, this new virus quickly spread throughout the capital city of Covidorne. The suburbs of Borebland, having successfully dealt with the 'vegan virus' would be savagely decimated by the effects of this more potent one – and an aura of pandemonium soon followed.

11 Pandemic Pandemonium

Just as a sense of normality had returned in Borebland, a new mysterious virus was now sweeping throughout the world and from continent to continent.

Up until this point, the island nation of Austrutopia was relatively unscathed but that was soon about to change!

The Austrutopian government decided not to close all the borders immediately and, thus, the mysterious virus quickly made its way via airport terminals and several major seaports throughout the country.

In next to no time, numerous media platforms (print, visual and social) sensationalised this new worldwide phenomenon and collectively categorised it as *pandemic pandemonium.*

Throughout Borebland Shire, large batches of newsletters were being handed out to cyclists and pedestrians, mainly by Outdoor Dwellers Association (ODA) members who would enthusiastically scream, 'Pandemic pandemonium... read all about it!'

The local media soon saturated their audiences and readers with seemingly non-stop 'informative' propaganda.

The first few pages of the Borebland Pravda newspaper focused primarily on anything related to the new pandemic phenomena, no matter how bizarrely trivial it was.

Similarly, Fabrication News Channel One (FNC1), owned by the Borebland Shire Council, was euphorically fixated by the 'pandemic pandemonium' as well.

Every news timeslot was overwhelmingly dominated by the latest developments of this new and *treacherous* global phenomenon. Special news events were hastily broadcasted to provide even further saturation of the current situation. But, alas, worse was soon to follow – state politics soon entered the hysterical furore.

Inside the concreted and dreary-looking state parliament house, located at 666 Autumn Parade (Covidorne CBD), the supreme state commander (Premier Dandrogyni) addressed a packed media conference of over-zealous news reporters and camera operators alike. Commonly referred to as *Dear Leader*, he declared an overbearing and paternalistic list of 'safety' measures to be implemented immediately.

The gangly, bespectacled, half-bearded and cross-dressing Premier Dandrogyni (affectionately referred to as 'Dandi' by state-owned media groups) calmly announced the following *guidelines of empathy*, effective from midnight:

1. Every individual was only allowed to travel within a radius of five kilometres from their home address.

2. Each individual will only be able to exercise outdoors for a maximum of one hour per day, either on their own or with one other person.

3. Only one 'healthy' person from a household was allowed to purchase essentials (e.g. groceries and medicines) in an indoor setting and no more than twice a week.

4. All schools and non-essential businesses were to be temporarily closed.

Premier Dandrogyni stressed, however, that these 'follow the science' measures were only meant to be a guideline. He further added that local shire councils were free to implement their *own* empathetic rules and regulations of 'communal kindness'.

All of Luzerstan's shire councils implemented and enforced the state government's new guidelines immediately.

A few of the state's shires (all located within Covidorne) decided to implement further and harsher restrictions. Then there was the Borebland Shire Council!

Three days after the state's 'safety measures' had been implemented, the Borebland Shire Council introduced even more draconian rules.

Beginning with the implementation of over-the-top travel restrictions, all vehicles (except for essential deliveries) were banned from using any of the public roads within Borebland.

Secondly, *time-measured* zones were hastily introduced. There would be ten-minute time slots for cyclists and twenty-minute time slots for those travelling on foot, but only for travelling to and from places of employment or shopping for essential items such as grocery items, alcoholic/non-alcoholic beverages, and medicines.

Borebland Shire Council then decided to 'mandate' the wearing of face masks (wholly covering the nose and mouth) by everyone as soon as they left their place of residence.

Several days later, boxes were delivered to one of the council's chamber rooms, all paid by locally raised taxes (council rates, congestion tax, vehicle privilege tax, etc.).

A large number of unlabelled boxes (containing 500–1000 light-blue coloured facemasks) were immediately made available to all of Borebland's residents.

After a short but successful period of lobbying by several community groups, notably the Witchy Bitches Femo Club (WBFC) and the Warring Vegans Social Club (WVSC), the Green Gaia supremo proudly announced on FNC1 that *full-faced* plastic shields had been ordered and should arrive within the next several days.

According to the extremist elements of the WBFC and the WVSC, the wearing of the face mask alone did not offer sufficient protection!

Within the next few days, a bizarre competition was seemingly taking place in the streets, along walkways, in shopping centres and even supermarket aisles in many parts of Borebland.

Whilst the standard blue-coloured 'face muzzle' (as coined by the Beef and Beer Bogan Pride Association) was the preferred option, local artists (and aspiring ones as well) sought to make an extra source of income by creating colourful and often bizarre images on the masks.

As requested by local members and affiliates of several artistic movements, many unlabelled boxes of white-coloured masks soon arrived, all arranged and paid for by the Borebland Shire Council.

In next to no time, a substantial portion of the local population was wearing an intriguing array of colourful, image-based facial masks.

Rainbow-coloured ones with a beaming image of the Green Gaia (in the middle of the design) were one of the most favoured. The opened mouths of rottweilers or pit bulls were another favourite, along with prison cell bars – just to name a few.

Both blue and white coloured masks with 'meaningful' slogans were also popular. Strangely though, a small section of the community strived to take the madness to even further heights.

The mandatory wearing of a face mask outside the home though, simply wasn't enough for a small outlandish but quite irritating section of the community, who sadly wanted to be further 'protected' by even more extreme measures.

Full-faced plastic shields that also covered face masks were soon gaining in popularity, particularly in crowded or semi-crowded areas such as in supermarkets, on public transport or sections of footpaths with high pedestrian numbers. But even worse was to follow!

A small number of individuals, who became known locally as *self-protection extremists*, decided to fully protect themselves from head to toe – in plastic.

Yellow-coloured wet weather gear was a popular choice of full-body armour, but other ideas soon emerged as well. For example, the improvised and innovative use of black-coloured garbage bags or sheets of thick plastic was soon on display in indoor and outdoor settings. The eccentricities, however, didn't stop there.

The local media soon 'jumped on the bandwagon' and deliberately sensationalised other zany ideas being put into practice.

To combat the dire effects of this seemingly plague-like virus sweeping throughout the Borebland shire, a few of these 'self-protection' extremists had decided to use several types of breathing apparatuses.

Scuba diving equipment such as masks, air hoses and oxygen tanks had been modified to cover their heads (and necks). Several individuals even wore breathing apparatuses that were uncannily similar to ones worn by wartime fighter jet pilots!

Later, another strange trend began to emerge – colourful and imaginative 'one-metre zone' hula hoops. These plastic or wooden hoops were artistically modified so that no one could get within a metre of the enthusiastic wearer who would gleefully wander aimlessly and quite provocatively within a crowded area.

The popular global phenomenon of *safe distancing* (where individuals were regularly encouraged to keep their distance from each other) had now been in place for several weeks.

Charlie, Lazer and others began to wonder if these *hula hoop warriors* were being sponsored by the 'wacky baccy' element of the Borebland Shire Council!

As the number of 'virus victims' continued to rise, the Luzerstan government decided to implement a bizarre and highly controversial plan.

In a sustained effort to control the introduced virus, the government decided to cordon the outward boundaries of Covidorne off from the rest of the state.

A 'Ring of Steel' (a term coined by a national newspaper) was created. Roadblocks were installed on major arterial roads leading out of the city, all patrolled by a joint operation between the state police force and federal military personnel.

Extra surveillance was hastily installed. Cameras and low-flying drones now dominated the landscape in and around the militarised checkpoints.

Not to be outdone, however, the Borebland Shire Council, charismatically and fervently led by the Green Gaia, decided to set up *their* version of a 'ring of steel'.

Using an over-the-top and blatant maternalistic approach, the council reassured the shire's residents by repeatedly stating (as enthusiastically reported and endorsed by the Borebland Pravda and the FNC1 television station): 'We are THE council of empathy. We will endeavour to protect everyone from nasty outside influence – at any cost.'

Roadblocks, along with checkpoints were quickly set up, encircling all of Borebland Shire. The roadblocks consisted of steel bollards and what uncannily looked like large wooden pommel horses.

To lighten the mood of these barricaded areas, local artists were soon invited by the Green Gaia to paint or decorate these pommel horses and bollards in a manner widely portrayed as 'flamboyant enlightenment'.

The artists, in turn, were well compensated for their efforts, primarily funded by local ratepayers but also through local donations where gold coin (and small-value banknotes) donations were generously bestowed upon them as they *passionately* performed their 'artistic duties' on the streets.

The checkpoints were patrolled by a specially appointed law enforcement taskforce, consisting entirely of members of several local bicycle gangs (particularly the Pinkerton Mob).

This specially-appointed group was easily recognisable by their full-body black Lycra, along with a pair of rainbow-coloured armbands worn on the top part of each sleeve. On the back of their Lycra tops, the words 'SPECIAL OPS' were written in a bold red colour.

The process and creation of this special operations task force were organised by the Borebland Shire Council under the ever-maternalistic direction of the Green Gaia, all paid for by a seemingly ever-present pool of local taxation finances.

But, alas, life for the average Borebland resident was just to become even more uncomfortable!

In an even more bizarre attempt to further control the 'despicable' virus, the Green Gaia decided to implement what would be commonly known throughout the rest of the world as *martial law.*

Local media outlets, however, soon branded the new law as an 'emergency power'.

Borebland Shire initially endured a 30-day lockdown, along with a nightly curfew between 10:00 p.m. and 5:00 a.m.

The 'mandated' (as opposed to being lawful) wearing of facial masks outside one's residence remained. Significantly, it was now enforced more rigorously than ever before.

Ever-present and vigilant compliance officers purposefully strode along the streets, in shopping centres (especially in supermarkets), in and out of cafes/restaurants/hotels – and even in parks and children's playgrounds.

Strangely enough, cyclists and joggers were exempt from having to wear face masks whilst riding or running. They did, however, have to wear one if they stopped (or walked) at any time.

Instead of putting the mask on and taking it off regularly, the majority of them would just wear it under their chin. As a result, joggers and cyclists soon became known as *energised chin-nappy wearers*.

Motorists (and their passengers) also had to wear a face mask – even if they were driving alone.

The words 'compliance' and 'caring' soon became well-known buzzwords, extensively used by local print and visual media personnel.

In nearly every visual interview or printed article, these two buzzwords were consistently overused by the Green Gaia supremo and her fellow Borebland councillors.

Parroted phrases such as: 'We care for our residents'; 'We're here to help everyone get through this unprecedented crisis'; and 'We must have empathy for friends and family through loving acts of compliance' soon led to the Borebland Shire Council commencing an actively aggressive campaign.

A campaign that would encourage (and forcibly persuade) the compliant residents to ridicule those who did not strictly adhere to the Green Gaia's dictatorial directives!

A controversial *Dob-in-Hotline* was set up, resulting in the community swiftly evolving into a very divided one. Even in the Spirit of Wokeness residential complex, Floozie tried to enforce these measures of 'barbaric' compliance.

The female residents were mostly quite contented to just comply with the official rules and directives as set out by the Borebland Shire Council.

The male residents were less inclined to comply. Lazer especially. Charlie and the other two male tenants (Alek and Frank), however, would occasionally ignore or flaunt the rules (or directives) by venturing into other nearby suburbs, either to exercise or just to visit friends, outside the twenty-minute walking zone.

Additionally, all four male tenants refused to wear face masks in any of the corridors of the complex or even outside the building at times.

Charlie, though, would occasionally wear a face mask in a crowded situation such as in a supermarket or on a busy tram but Lazer refused to wear one and was regularly confronted and occasionally arrested by compliance officers.

Over several months, Lazer received a hefty number of fines but refused to pay any of them. Eighteen months later, he took the matter of unpaid fines to a courtroom. The fines were sensationally dropped as the magistrate ruled that the issuing of them by overzealous compliant officers was deemed to be unlawful!

Despite the male tenants rarely adhering to the directives and rules of the authorities, Floozie decided not to inform law enforcement agencies of their acts of non-compliance.

Floozie, however, often chastised all four of them at any given opportunity. Frank, Alek, and Charlie generally responded to her with a smile and then moved casually away from her, returning to their respective units.

A turbulent and forthright Lazer was far less tactful and, thus, was hostile towards Floozie at times. A war of words between the pair quickly erupted!

The 'promised' thirty-day lockdown soon developed into one that lasted more than ninety days!

The Ring of Steel was eventually lifted and as it coincided with a university holiday break, Charlie decided to drive to his hometown of Ratatatatutra.

Initially, he had planned to stay there for only two weeks. A week later, however, the number of virus cases had risen significantly and without warning, the *Dear Leader* (Premier Dandrogyni) decided to reinstall the widely hated Ring of Steel around the city of Covidorne once more.

As a result, Charlie ended up spending the next six weeks in Ratatatatutra and, thus, continued his course online using his father's PC (personal computer) – and free Wi-Fi.

The second 'Ring of Steel' was eventually lifted but before returning to Covidorne, Charlie had to download a re-entry permit online and print a hard copy.

Just as Charlie entered Covidorne, he was stopped at a roadblock and was bluntly told to *'show us your permission to travel document'* by a 'power-hungry buffoon' dressed in all-black attire, wearing a distinguishable red and green armband on his upper left sleeve.

This *bizarre* and *abnormal* way of life would continue for six more months. After this time, normality slowly began to return. Charlie had completed just over half of his bachelor's degree in information technology at the University of Woke and Knowledge.

Despite enjoying the inner-suburban life of Covidorne for the past two years or so, Charlie's recent six-week stay in Ratatatatutra persuaded him to re-evaluate his future life path options. The largely unplanned and extended taste of rural living had stirred up certain emotions within him!

12 Caught Between Two Worlds

Several times a year, Charlie would drive his ageless but ever-reliable Land Rover from the 'dazzling lights' of Hiptoun to his serene and blissful birthplace of Ratatatatutra.

Cruising quite casually along the dual-carriage freeway and in the left lane, he drove at a speed of no more than ninety-five kilometres per hour, well within the 110-kilometre-per-hour speed limit zone.

After driving for several hours, Charlie turned off the freeway and travelled along several lesser-used roads; ones having plenty of recently-filled potholes, eroded (or missing) edges and were quite narrow in several sections. Welcome to rural Luzerstan!

The drive of just over four hundred kilometres usually took Charlie between five and six hours, depending on the conditions of the roads at the time.

Eventually, he arrived at a closed farm gate. After passing through and closing it, Charlie continued along a single-lane dirt road for several hundred metres before bringing his vehicle to a halt near the spacious front lawn of a 19th-century-built homestead: the family home.

A few minutes later, Charlie was seated at the kitchen table, chatting incessantly with his parents and two younger siblings.

As Charlie chatted away, he scoffed down recently home-made scones, topped with homemade strawberry jam, and whipped thick cream, along with homemade plain biscuits and several fresh-brewed cups of tea, poured from a decades-old floral-themed teapot.

Charlie mostly used these holiday breaks for relaxation purposes, along with meeting up with family members and former school friends.

During the first and third two-week breaks, however, he needed to allocate sufficient time to progress with course-related assignments or prepare for upcoming mini-exams. The due date for an assignment or a mini-exam (for example) would be within the first two weeks of the next semester.

Other assignments required a substantial number of hours and thus, Charlie would need to use some of the semester break time to complete the necessary tasks on time.

Nevertheless, Charlie still managed to spend a healthy part of his time outdoors, mostly to assist other family members with the everyday chores of farm and orchard life.

The main chores included: pruning fruit trees; cleaning irrigation treacles; installing irrigation treacles and pipes; collecting hens' eggs; and even cattle mustering.

Outside the farm and orchard life, Charlie would regularly catch up and socialise with people he had previously known either through school, sport, or part-time employment.

During the various holiday breaks of the first university year, Charlie was still able to 'connect' with most residents of Ratatatatutra (and the surrounding areas) at a level that could described as being on a similar wavelength to them.

By the end of the year though, and especially throughout the first eight-week summer break, Charlie sensed that the camaraderie between him and a sizeable proportion of the local population was beginning to wane.

In the past, Charlie had been engaged in mostly 'agreeable' conversations with the local population, particularly when discussing topics such as politics, environmental issues or even the behaviour of sporting celebrities.

Strangely enough, as he spent an increasing amount of time in the 'Big Smoke', Charlie found himself disagreeing with a large portion of the residents of Ratatatatutra (and nearby towns), particularly with a trivial detail of a particular point or points of a discussion.

Occasionally, someone would wryly suggest to Charlie that he had 'changed'. The problem, however, was that *he had changed* – but they had not.

Charlie now regarded the local populace as largely being 'uniformly like-minded'. They, in turn, would never accept his exposure to a new world that was deemed as one of mostly 'woke and progressive enlightenment'.

Nevertheless, whenever Charlie returned to visit the 'good folk' of Ratatatatutra, cordial and harmonious relationships remained, despite disagreements over certain topical details.

Strangely though, he started to resonate more positively with younger individuals. Many of them were in their teens and were either still at school or were recent school leavers, undecided about their future life prospects.

Whenever Charlie attempted to share or discuss his newly discovered 'woke' inner-suburban experiences with his family and former school, working or sporting colleagues, he was often met with scorn and cynicism.

The diehard 'country bumpkins' often ridiculed (but light-heartedly) him with the lines: 'What happened to you Charlie, are you now a city slicker?' or 'Don't forget your roots... eh, Charlie!'

Meanwhile, many of the local youngsters were seemingly quite intrigued by Charlie's new *awakening experiences* and in response, displayed a curious sense of interest in Charlie's world of 'adventurous and educated' progressiveness.

Charlie soon realised that many of these youngsters were dissatisfied with their present and mundane rustic lifestyle. Even several of his old school friends rarely ever returned to Ratatatatutra as they had settled well into their new choice of lifestyle, often many kilometres away.

During the first summer break in Ratatatatutra, Charlie spent a considerable amount of time outdoors, enjoying the fresh and tranquil air of several small orchards, along with his parents' farm (and orchard) as well.

The nearby 'tin-pot' towns of Mordopeyeh and Hardgrona provided him with a source of occasional employment whether it be picking fruit (cherries, apricots, peaches, and pears), apple thinning and even a bit of summer pruning.

It was a welcomed change for Charlie as he appreciated the 'therapeutic' air of the orchard immensely – quite different from the hustle and bustle of the inner-city suburban lifestyle.

Throughout Charlie's first year of study, he relished the new-found lifestyle within the Borebland shire, especially in the suburbs of Hiptoun, Bunnslich and South Duffel.

The ever-present sub-culture of woke and progressiveness within this area of Covidorne certainly influenced his changed state of mind; one that could now be deemed as being far more 'socially aware.'

By the second year, the novelty of 'social awareness' was now being questioned by Charlie. Although his relationships with family and friends in Ratatatatutra had moved towards a different direction, he had decided not to forget his roots either.

The therapeutic nature of rustic life when working in an orchard or farm, prompted Charlie to question himself from time to time about where his future might lie. By the third year of his studies, he now began to feel that city life may not be part of the next phase of his life.

Whilst Charlie enjoyed making new friendships and being an active participant in the vibrant social life of Borebland Shire, certain characteristics of the 'thought processes' by many of the Shire's residents had also irked him. Especially within the last twelve months.

One characteristic trait (of the Shire's residents) that had greatly irked Charlie was the 'air of superiority' displayed by a high percentage of the city-born residents towards their supposed lower-status country 'cousins' – especially from several of the larger community-spirited groups such as the Witchy Bitches Femo Club (WBFC) and the Warring Vegans Social Club (WVSC).

In the latter half of Charlie's third year of study, the WVSC (along with members of the WBFC as well) had noticeably stepped up their *Meat is Murder* campaign, through what they self-termed as an 'integrity crusade.' On several occasions, they had targeted beef producers and poultry farmers in rural areas of Luzerstan.

Besides camping illegally on a tract of farmland, the group would verbally and physically harass meat-producing farmers and their families, either outside their homes or in cattle yards/sheds/mini abattoirs.

Armed with visual and sound recording equipment, the *unruly mobs* also harassed business owners and customers in nearby small towns, particularly outside butcher shops and inside supermarkets. They would often live-stream but later upload edited content to various social media platforms.

Then, one day in early February of the following year, the group decided to target Ratatatatutra!

One afternoon, Charlie was driving through Ratatatatutra when he noticed a small group of scruffily dressed individuals loitering casually just outside the post office.

Their bohemian-like dress sense had caught Charlie's attention. After doing a U-turn, he slowly drove past the group and instantly recognised several of them!

Further down the main street, Charlie parked his vehicle near the Ratatatatutra Hotel. He knew that some local cattle and poultry farmers (and several orchardists) would be there.

Within a few minutes, the local 'bush telegraph' was underway and soon in full operation mode. Within an hour, farming communities in and around Ratatatatutra were now aware of the possibility of vegan extremists gate-crashing their farms and businesses.

During this time, the publican of the hotel, Ted Pulpitt, had been in contact with highway patrol officers, who soon spotted and pulled over two rainbow-coloured minibuses. *WVSC Touring Company* was written on both sides of each bus. Both vehicles were full of 'unkempt-looking' passengers.

The officers informed Ted (the publican) that the buses were still about eighty kilometres away from Ratatatatutra.

He, in turn, informed the hotel's patrons that an *ingenious* plan would soon be underway!

Twelve kilometres south of Ratatatatutra, roadblock signs were hastily set up by a group of farmers falsely stating that due to 'bridge damage' the road was now closed.

One of the farmers, Karl 'Psycho' Manson, decided to open a tract of his farming land for 'free camping' and erected a sign just before the roadblock barriers. The ingenious plan was to direct the two minibuses to this tract of land so that the large group could set up a camp for the night.

Based on the previous incidents of illegal camping within various farming communities, the group of locals suspected that the 'undesirables' more than likely had tents and camping equipment on the buses.

About an hour later, along with waning daylight, the two minibuses came upon the roadblock. Karl greeted them and a few minutes later, the two bus drivers were directed to the camping area on his property.

The cleared area was also near a dam and a small row of trees containing several stone fruits: plums, nectarines, and peaches. Karl stated to the now-weary bunch of activists, that the dam was suitable for bathing and to help themselves to the delicious fruit.

With a wry but sinister smile, Karl wished them a good night's sleep and further added that the 'bridge' would be fully repaired sometime tomorrow. Little did they know, the vegan *activist warriors* were in for quite a nasty surprise early the next morning!

As the vegan activists gathered around a large campfire that evening smoking joints and drinking cheap alcohol, a large number of farmers and orchardists from several small farming communities had gathered inside the Ratatatatutra Hotel. Several police officers were also present.

The group of farmers and orchardists were planning to ambush the campsite, just as dawn was breaking the next morning. The plan of attack was meticulously planned over the next couple of hours or so!

Just before 5:00 a.m. the next morning, a large 'posse' of residents (farmers, orchardists, business owners and others) led by several large tractors with enclosed cabins (to protect the safety of the drivers) swarmed the campsite. Two of the tractors were each towing a large canister.

Speaker systems had been set up on top of the enclosed cabins of several of the other tractors. Numbering more than a hundred (with many of them armed with rifles or semi-automatics), the large 'posse' marched towards the *derelict-looking* campsite.

With the use of a bullhorn, Karl bellowed: 'Wakey, wakey children… get up, pack your gear AND get off my property!'

Within a couple of minutes, most of the brain-fogged activists had emerged from their tents. Several of them, now armed with steel bars and baseball bats, approached the large group who were mostly standing behind the two tractors towing canisters.

The drivers of the two tractors then drove towards the armed delinquents before veering away from them with the right side of the canister now facing the unruly bunch.

Suddenly, the canisters were turned on, showering the would-be attackers with a mixture of manure and water. They quickly retreated. Karl continued: 'You've got less than half an hour to pack up and leave... or we start shooting!'

Twenty-five minutes later, the rainbow-coloured buses slowly drove past the large and noisy local 'lynching mob'.

Charlie, with an unloaded rifle resting over his shoulder, was thoroughly enjoying the bizarre spectacle!

Karl 'Psycho' Manson was still bellowing through the loud hailer: 'Hope you enjoyed your free overnight stay, but don't ever come back to this area again!'

As the buses approached the main road, the locals pointed their mostly unloaded weapons over the buses and several sound systems (on top of several of the tractors) were turned on, delivering a continual noise of loud and steady gunfire, as if they were in a war zone.

The activists instantly reacted with loud hysterical screaming and both bus drivers suddenly applied more pressure on the accelerator pedals!

The buses, however, were blocked by police vehicles (with red and blue lights flashing) in front of the roadblock barriers.

They informed the bus drivers that two police vehicles would follow them for the first fifty or so kilometres of the journey back to Covidorne.

One of the officers, menacingly, reminded them not to come back to the area. He further added: 'If you try this stunt again, my fellow officers will just stand by and let the well-armed locals sort you scruffy lot out!'

This incident was a significant turning point for Charlie, deciding there and then that he would only stay in Covidorne to complete his bachelor's degree in information technology.

Charlie completed his course nine months later in early November. For the past two years, he had been mentally caught between two contrasting worlds – rural versus city.

Charlie, however, now knew where his heart and mind truly belonged.

13 Goodbye Big Smoke, Hello Wanderlust

During the latter half of Charlie's fourth year of study, he often contemplated what the future might have in store for him once his bachelor's degree in information technology (specialising in business information systems) course had been completed.

As the final exams period neared (commencing in early November), Charlie decided that he would bring his life-changing period of 'cultural awakening experiences' to a glorious end and return to Ratatatatutra in early December.

By now, Charlie was eager to leave the dazzling lights of the big city behind and return to an idyllic rural lifestyle; one that was carefree and of a simpler nature. Firstly, though, he needed to pass all his exams.

Charlie prepared and studied hard for his final exams which were conducted over two weeks. Besides passing his exams easily, he would achieve mostly excellent results in all subjects undertaken.

Charlie did not need to repeat any assignments or have to re-sit any exams but would still have to wait until the end of January to receive his official bachelor's degree in information technology.

In the last week of January, Charlie received official confirmation that he had completed his bachelor's degree in information technology.

Four years of consistent study, along with 'woke and progressive enlightenment' was finally over!

Besides his newly-acquired degree certification, Charlie had also collected quite a few extra 'pieces of paper' (minor certificates) during this period: woke and progressive politics; craft beer brewing; protest banner design and development – just to name a few.

At the time, Charlie was only concerned with what lay ahead for his immediate future. For the next five months, he was contented to just indulge in farm and orchard work on his parent's property.

Charlie would also pick fruit at nearby orchards ranging from three to seven days a week. Many years, however, would elapse before he decided to finally enter the information technology (IT) world in the form of full-time employment.

Once the apple-picking season (mid-March to the end of May) had finished, Charlie decided to purchase a small 6x4 trailer, along with a large canvas tent and many items of camping equipment.

Charlie departed from his parent's property in the first week of June and drove his ever-reliable Land Rover along a series of roads, from quality-made highways to unsealed rural roads and throughout the three eastern states of Austrutopia. Five days later, he met up with an old friend: Lazer.

In June of the previous year, Lazer suddenly decided one day to leave the city of Covidorne altogether. Two days after informing Charlie and several of the other complex building residents of his rash decision, he loaded his grey multiple-dented Toyota Camry with two large fully laden backpacks, a smaller backpack and several plastic supermarket bags filled with assorted items such as cutlery, plates, cups, etc.

It was later learnt that Lazer had been contemplating and planning to *hit the road* for several weeks. He too (like Charlie) had wished to leave behind the dazzling lights of Covidorne and, thus, begin a new lifestyle – an itinerant fruit-picking one. His long-term goal was to work and travel throughout Austrutopia for at least the next few years.

Twelve months later, Lazer crossed paths with Charlie again, in the northern state of Queening (commonly known as the state 'where the sun shines out of everything'). At the time, he was picking oranges near the small inland town of Lossbah.

After setting up his tent on a campsite (inside the orchard), Charlie commenced orange picking the following day. He would work with Lazer, sharing the use of a tractor.

The tractor towed four trailers with three large wooden bins on each trailer. They took turns driving the tractor as they steadily moved along a double row of orange trees.

Once all twelve bins were filled, one of them would take the fully laden tractor (and trailers) back to the packing shed and bring another tractor, with empty bins, back to the rows where they were picking.

A significant advantage of being employed in this orchard was the availability of free accommodation. Besides having several dongers (demountable buildings each consisting of several rooms), an area of powered sites was available for those with personal accommodation means such as caravans, camper trailers, campervans, or tents.

Charlie had pitched his tent on a powered site whilst Lazer was residing in one of the donger rooms. The pair would work together for about six weeks.

Seven months earlier, Charlie had been undergoing the first phase of preparing for the next chapter in his life. By the last week of November, he had already resigned from his part-time brewery job and for a couple of weeks, Charlie had been farewelling former workmates, university friends (along with several lecturers/tutors), trivia team members (and even rivals from other teams) and of course, fellow residents in the Spirit of Wokeness building complex.

On the day of Charlie's departure from Hiptoun (and with a tint of sadness), he loaded his ageless Land Rover with his belongings. Alek and Frank assisted him in carrying heavy and bulkier items from his unit to the vehicle.

After a lengthy chat with Alek and Frank, Charlie drove out of the underground car park and several minutes later, was driving along Kiddenee Road.

Charlie was leaving behind a four-year experience of 'woke and progressive enlightenment' in exchange for a soon-to-be idyllic rustic lifestyle: one that was much slower and oozed simplicity.

Eight months later, a rejuvenated and *sun-tanned* Charlie was blissfully toiling away in an orange orchard. As he worked tirelessly, he regularly contemplated the thought of adopting an itinerant lifestyle within Austrutopia, along with travelling and working in other countries for at least the next several years.

For the next few years, Charlie rarely ventured anywhere near Covidorne. When he did drive to the capital, however, it was only for short-time visits within the Borebland shire and mostly in the suburb of Hiptoun.

Though Charlie had enjoyed living in the 'big smoke' for almost four years, his new-found level of motivation was now geared towards a new-found *wanderlust spirit*; one that would be primarily fuelled by an itinerant fruit-picking lifestyle!

About the Author

P.J. Kropp was born in Orange, New South Wales (Australia).

After completing a Diploma in Education certificate in Sydney in late 1987, P.J. Kropp decided not to enter the teaching profession the following year. Instead, he returned to his birthplace and commenced fruit-picking (cherries) employment in one of the numerous orchards in the district of Orange, a move that ultimately led to an itinerant lifestyle that would last for more than twenty years.

In May 1990, P.J. Kropp boarded a one-way flight to London and, thus, began his overseas *wanderlust* journey.

In June 2008, P.J. Kropp farewelled the itinerant lifestyle (and wanderlust journey) and relocated to Melbourne, Victoria. At the age of forty-three, P.J. Kropp was a full-time student once more!

P.J. Kropp completed his bachelor's degree in information technology (Business Information Systems) in 2014 and the following year, commenced two literary projects: 'The Itinerant Way' and 'Travelling Below the Surface'.

The Itinerant Way was published in October 2019, whilst Travelling Below the Surface was published in April 2021.

P.J. Kropp began writing 'Welcome to Hiptoun' in May 2021.